THE
LONG SLIDE

THE
LONG SLIDE

STORIES

JAMES GRAINGER

ECW PRESS   M I S F I T

Published by ECW PRESS
2120 Queen Street East, Suite 200, Toronto, Ontario, Canada M4E 1E2

NATIONAL LIBRARY OF CANADA CATALOGUING IN PUBLICATION

Grainger, James, 1965–
The long side / James Grainger.

Short stories.
ISBN 1-55022-677-0

1. Men — Fiction. I. Title.

PS8613.R335L65 2004   C813'.6   C2004-902604-6

Editor: Michael Holmes/a misFit book
Cover design : Bill Douglas at The Bang
Author photo: Mary Williamson
Text design and production: Mary Bowness
Typesetting: Marijke Friesen
Printing: Marc Veilleux

This book is set in Janson.

The publication of *The Long Slide* has been generously
supported by the Canada Council, the Ontario Arts Council, the Ontario Media
Development Corporation, and the Government of Canada through
the Book Publishing Industry Development Program. Canada

DISTRIBUTION
CANADA: Jaguar Book Group, 100 Armstrong Avenue, Georgetown, ON, L7G 5S4

PRINTED AND BOUND IN CANADA

ECW PRESS
ecwpress.com

For Nathan

I know this is paradise

Everyone old has dreamed of all their lives —
Bonds and gestures pushed to one side
Like an outdated combine harvester,
And everyone young going down the long slide

To happiness, endlessly.

"High Windows," Philip Larkin

CONTENTS

ACKNOWLEDGMENTS

Every first-time author has a long list of people to thank. My list includes Michael, Jack, Emily, and everyone at ECW for their hard work and patience. Amy and Jen for getting things rolling. Pamela, Janie, Rob, Jana, Derek, Ross, Darren, Joseph, Larry, Christine, Matt, and everyone else who gave editorial advice and encouragement. Bill and Mary for their design acumen. The good folks at Quill for giving me the time off. Special thanks to Tracey, Alison, Nicole, and B.W. Powe. Biggest thanks to Petra.

Thanks as well to the citizens of Toronto and Ontario for their support through the Toronto Arts Council and the Ontario Arts Council.

THE LONG SLIDE

Patrick saw Amy Phillips standing in front of the bakery eating an ice-cream cone. Amy was seventeen. She stood alone in the heat in shorts and a light blue T-shirt and a ridiculous red visor, resting her weight on one leg. She would have just finished school last week, the rest of the summer stretching out before her like a big cat sleeping in the sun.

Amy was a friend of Jeff Bergman's younger sister, a connection that eventually drew Patrick and Amy into the same party circles. Jeff said that Amy was a tease who pretended not to know how sexy she was. Patrick decided that Amy knew how sexy she was, but wasn't sure how she felt about this gift or how she wanted to put it to use. She was more beautiful than most of the girls at the parties they went to but she always looked as if she'd just thrown on a set of her older brother's hand-me-downs. Patrick started teasing her at parties, casting her as the hopeless straight to his druggie bohemian. Amy would tell him that she wasn't as straight as he thought and leave it at that. They both got off on the teasing. The jokes confirmed a secret vision that Patrick was cultivating of himself as a wise and lovingly grumpy man who was ready for bigger things than his own bad habits. He noticed that Amy was more enthusiastic and goofy around him than she was with her girlfriends, as if the limited role his teasing cast her in gave her licence to be her true self.

This game was bothering Brenda. She would stand on the other side of the room ripping phantom pieces of paper in her hands as she pretended not to watch him talking to Amy, and then give him the silent treatment later, trying to freeze an explanation or apology out of him. Patrick wouldn't play that game. He wasn't doing anything wrong. People flirted, it was natural. Everyone did it, everyone but Brenda. Patrick wished that Brenda would flirt with someone — it excited him to think about another man trying to pick her up, only to be humiliated when she went home with Patrick at the end of the night.

Patrick had thought his life was under control. He had gotten an apartment downtown and a job that he didn't hate, and he still came up to North York on the weekends to party with Brenda and his old friends from high school. Brenda was finishing Grade 13 and getting ready for university. He did something nice for her 18th birthday and Valentine's Day, though the dates were only three days apart. But every time Patrick saw Amy at a party it took him that much longer to stop thinking about her. For days afterwards he would catch himself imagining that he was on a date with Amy, not Brenda, or that it was Amy's house he was dropping by after work and *her* parents he was hanging out with. Amy always scored higher in these comparison tests — she was more fun and laughed more often and was open to new experiences. She didn't read into what Patrick was saying or blame him for thinking things that had never occurred to him.

Patrick vowed to stop fantasizing about Amy, at least when Brenda was with him. He couldn't. He worried whether Amy would show up at a party he was going to. He even began to choose which parties to go to based on the odds of Amy's attendance. Brenda knew that something was eating at him, but when she asked him if he was okay he said he was just getting tired of seeing the same people all the time. He said he was restless, and if Brenda pressed him to elaborate he would say there was nothing wrong with being restless, she should try it herself some time. When Amy didn't show up at a party, Patrick would brood and drink too much. Brenda would ask him what was wrong and he'd say he just wanted to go home, he was sick of these people. When Amy did show up, Patrick became the king of the party. All of his jokes and stories were pitched for Amy to overhear — they were the sirens calling her to his island. And Amy *would* drift over and join the circle that formed around Patrick when he was in a good mood at a party. He would trade insults with his friends, deliberately leaving Amy out of the teasing to set her apart from everyone else. Even with his eyes closed his body would have known where she was in the room, how many steps it would take to reach her. He felt his body straining against the performance he put on for her and his friends, and this feeling of restraining his body gave Patrick even more power.

In the spring he saw Amy at a party. Brenda was out with her friends at a birthday dinner and was coming to the party later. Because there was no one to interrupt them, they got past the teasing and Amy began to tell him about her family. Patrick showed her the long scar on his forehead he'd gotten when he was a kid. She prodded the scar where it rose into a low, smooth ridge and said "Oh!" as if the flesh had moved under her fingertip. Patrick asked Amy to dance — God, they were at a party where people danced.

He started dancing with her and that Adam Ant song came on: "Don't drink, don't smoke, what do you do?" Patrick hated Adam Ant, but he knew the words and he sang them to Amy as if the two of them were potential lovers in a musical and this was the number where he mocked her chastity. Amy, as a girl in a musical must, took the challenge and danced a little closer to him than a girl like her ought to.

She danced close enough for him to feel the heat coming off her, the smell of her scalp. He touched her arm and her arm went limp in his hand. She was as committed as he was to the roles this game imposed on them, even more so because her role demanded that she always be a half-step behind him, negotiating the momentum that he had put into motion. He pulled the slack from her arm and began to draw her closer, waiting for the recoiling jerk under his fingertips, but her arm stayed limp in his hand — she let it be the rope drawing her to him. He felt her body slacken against him, as if she were a volunteer in one of those trust exercises where someone falls blind backwards into the arms of someone standing behind them. She looked up at him. Her eyes were floating with specks of light. There was an even sheen of sweat on her face and neck. She might have just come home from an evening of working in an apple orchard. He could feel the strong, healthy life radiating from her. Her expression was expectant, nervous, even a little resentful that he was about to start this new thing in her life because her old life had been fine without him. There was a warning there, too, a sense that he would be punished if he took advantage of her trust. It was as if something inside her but not *of* her was warning him to stay away. Patrick could actually feel a physical force repelling him, as if a guardian animal, a half-awake bear or leopard, was nestled inside Amy waiting to maul any intruder who mistreated its charge. He fought against the accusation. He was in love with Amy. He wanted to start his whole life over again with her at his side. Amy saw Patrick's expression change. She saw the doubt there and it seemed to wound her. She pulled away from Patrick as if she were the one who had done something wrong. He told her that it was time for another drink, transforming the kiss that didn't happen into a joke, the final punchline to a long round of flirting. Amy tried to laugh, but Patick knew that he had humiliated her.

He left the party with Brenda but went to his apartment downtown alone. Lying in bed he kept running the scene with Amy through his imagination — the dancing, the game, her arm going limp in his hand, the look she gave him when she leaned against his body. He would return to that moment — when she had looked up at him waiting to be kissed — and try to change the outcome, but even in his fantasies he was repelled by the guardian animal inside Amy. He had been named as a man unworthy of a girl like Amy.

Patrick spent the next few days alone in his apartment smoking joints and reading Carl Jung and watching horror movies over meals of starchy foods. He called in sick to work. He told Brenda he was too sick to see her and then wouldn't answer the phone when it rang. Even his constitution changed. Any shift in his emotions brought a rapid acceleration of his heartbeat that drained the blood from his head, making him feel as if he was about to fall from a tall building. He had to stay calm. He had to stay distracted. He tried to fantasize about Amy but the guardian animal was in his head and wouldn't even let him think about her. Eventually Brenda came round and helped him clean up his apartment. He cried on her chest in bed one night, but he couldn't tell her why he felt so awful because he didn't really know. He only knew that he had to change his whole life. He couldn't tell Brenda this because his relationship with her was the first thing that had to change. He couldn't tell her that the only way he was going to get better was to break up with her.

Running into Amy that afternoon was no coincidence. It was a sign, Patrick didn't know of what. But he was on his way to finally tell Brenda that he wanted to break up with her and here was Amy hanging around the mall as if she was just waiting for something to happen. He shoved the last of a donut into his mouth. He wished he hadn't smoked that joint on the walk from the subway station. Looking at her, so poised with her ice cream in the sun, he couldn't believe that he had ever had any power over her.

Amy looked surprised to see Patrick at the mall. Standing close to her for the first time in almost three months wrenched his body away from him, as if he'd been pushed from behind. He asked her what kind of ice cream she was eating, and hearing her answer so quickly he shifted into his old role and asked if he could have some of her ice cream, only a bite. Amy's shoulders tensed, as if she had just noticed a kink in her neck, and because she was so comfortable in her body the gesture looked theatrical, a signal to the audience to pay attention.

"Are you high?" she asked.

He took this as a cue for further teasing and said, "Fuck yeah." She smiled, but Patrick felt the guardian animal inside her move into position. "Just a little," he backtracked, affecting a tone that implied boredom with his own life. His hands clenched the handle of a phantom weapon, a machete to cut the guardian animal down. Amy was still smiling, waiting for him to tease her about her ice cream or her clean blue T-shirt, but she was on guard against him. She was small and slightly muscular, which registered in his nerves as a sign of delicious self-control. Her firm muscles and curves hung tightly to her frame like a festoon of medals won in a campaign of will.

He looked in the window of the bakery. He wanted to say something that would make her look at him the way she had at the party. He wanted to say something as good as the smell of that bread. The bright store fronts looked out of place in the white sunlight and humidity and exhaust fumes. No wonder they didn't build outdoor malls anymore.

"These stores should all be under one roof," he said. "It's the natural order of things."

"It's like it's not right that all these products should be exposed to the elements," Amy said. "It's like leaving a book in the rain."

"Exactly," he said too loudly. "That's good. You just make that up?"

"No, I use it every Saturday. What about you?"

"I thought it up just for you. Better than flowers, which I can't afford anyway."

Amy laughed and dropped her shoulders. Maybe his failure to kiss her at the party meant something different to her, a sign of conflicted emotions. She might even think that he'd been too shy to go through with it, or that he wanted to get to her know her better before they kissed. Did people still do that?

"Did I tell you I'm moving out to the Coast in September?" he said. "I've got a job in Victoria and my uncle's got a farm I'm going to live at for awhile."

"Cool."

"I'm not moving there forever. I just need to get away for awhile, you know. I feel like I've done everything I can here." He pulled out the almost empty pockets of his jeans. They both laughed. "I've done so much."

"I read about you in the newspaper," she said.

"My first million?"

"I heard it was ten."

"And my scholarships?"

"I wept during your valedictorian speech last year."

It was easy to laugh. They might have been talking about someone they both used to know and felt a little sorry for.

He told her that he had to pass her house so why didn't he walk her home? Amy lived in a big house just off of Lawrence with her parents and two younger brothers. Her father was a professor. Patrick had never known anyone whose father was a professor, so he asked Amy what her father taught. She said psychology and told him a funny story about a group of teenage animal liberationists who had set three of her father's monkeys free. The monkeys must have spooked their liberators, because the monkeys were found trying to open a jar of banana peppers in the cafeteria kitchen. Her father figured in the anecdote first as a gentle buffoon, then resourceful when called to action, forgiving but firm when the culprits were apprehended. Patrick imagined her father telling the story at the dinner table and each of the siblings taking a position on the issue of animal research, none straying outside the spectrum of belief embodied in their parents.

Patrick and Amy stood on the Phillips' lawn, and because she was from a world where people talked about their fathers' careers she asked Patrick what his father did and then stood back to wait for him to match her funny story. Patrick had plenty of stories about his father, who managed a bar and had a little sideline holding bets for a bookie, but most of the stories ended with a drunken customer stepping out of line and receiving his comeuppance, usually in the form of a beating or verbal humiliation. Patrick loved these stories, the easy sympathy with the enforcers of the code his father lived by, but Amy had probably never met a man like his father.

"Let's move into the shade," he said, pointing to the evergreen tree that bordered her lawn. "I don't do so well in the sun. I *am* going to come back, you know," Patrick said. "There's something I have to do out there. I'm going on a quest."

She said she understood. There might have even been a note of admiration in her voice.

"I'm going out to the West Coast alone," he said to her, suppressing his friend Steve's role in his exodus. Patrick wanted his sundering from the past to sound absolute, monastic. He almost started to tell Amy that he had come to North York that afternoon to break up with Brenda. "I don't want anyone to come with me," he said. "I'm not even going to take myself along." He felt his point slip into obscurity. He didn't care. The thought of what Brenda was going to say to him when he broke the news made him want to sabotage whatever intimacy he'd won back with Amy. "It's like I wish I could just leave myself here," he said. "Do you ever feel that way, that you could leave yourself behind?"

"Oh yeah."

"No you don't."

Amy was gnawing a hole in the side of the cone. "It's my pipe," she said, sucking the ice cream through the hole. "Is this what a normal person does?" She laughed and actually rolled her eyes. Her complete lack of self-consciousness almost made Patrick groan. They were standing close to each other in the shade. A tree root under his feet was trying to tip him onto her. He could smell Amy — soap and hair smell. She seemed to take a step away from him without moving her feet and crossed her arms over her breasts. Had he been staring at them?

"I have a picture of an octopus on my bedroom wall," she said. "I put it up when I was twelve and wanted to be an ichthyologist. It comforts me, I don't know why. You know — all those arms. Is *that* normal? Sometimes I think I'm going to become one of those old ladies who lives with fifty cats." Again she laughed, a kind of barking noise that surprised her and made her laugh harder.

Patrick felt the muscles in his torso almost convulse around what he wanted to say to her. She was the most beautiful thing he'd ever seen. He fought it all down. "You should join the army," he said.

"I might have to if we move back to Israel."

"You're not really moving back to Israel?"

"Maybe in a year. I'd be finished high school by then anyway."

"I don't want you to, to move to Israel." He could say that much to her.

"You're moving to the West Coast," she said.

"For a while. I'll be back one day. I'll write you a letter."

"Oh, I love letters. No one sends letters anymore."

"I do, or I will. I'll probably have nothing else to do all day."

"No," she said, "you'll be busy in no time."

He wanted to tell her that busyness was what he most wanted to avoid, that the whole point of his journey was to find a silent place to sink down deep into himself, away from this city and all the things that he'd fucked up here. He projected himself into his future and it was all silence — the ocean, mossy trees, mountains, a sparse apartment, coarse meals served in oversized Japanese soup bowls. The pain of not being able to share this vision with her was like a fist moving up through his intestines to clench his heart. He could see every pine needle on the branches shading Amy and him, every gulley in the tree bark and every wad of dry sap. The clarity horrified him. He took down her address on the back of a banking stub and said that he had to get going, which made her laugh and crush his formality with a hug.

Soon Patrick was walking beside the low apartment buildings that housed the Hasidic Jews, most of them Soviet Bloc refugees rescued by synagogue fundraising drives and then beached on this rare stretch of cheap rentals. When he lived in North York he used to try and spot Hasidim walking the streets on weeknights, but they seemed to rise from the mists of Friday dusks and drift up to Lawrence in black overcoats and wide round hats that were all rim, like the mechanism of a top waiting to be spun by the hand of God. Patrick would be waiting for the sun to go down and a party to start somewhere and the Hasidim would suddenly appear. Patrick would shadow their pace from the other side of the street, feeding on the reigned-in excitement of the little beardless boys, feeling that together they were following parallel treks to ecstasy, the Hasidim walking the path of devotion and ritual, he of suffering and worldliness. At dusk artificial and natural light cancelled each other. Shadows didn't take. It all *meant* something. Then the Hasidim would pass under the heavy tree branches on the other side of Lawrence, past Amy's house, and turn right, toward a synagogue Patrick had never seen.

Their buildings were set far back from the road on long narrow lawns without trees or hedges, and on rainy nights the dull yellow streetlights and bright windows transformed the buildings into gaudy riverboats docked in impossibly tranquil black waters. Patrick used to watch from the street, waiting for figures to move behind the yellow windows, waiting for the Hasidim to cast off and sail their buildings down the street. This was Patrick's favourite illusion, worth the risk of pneumonia and police harassment.

He arrived at Brenda's building and walked across the visitor's parking lot to the fenced-off pool. It was a miserable place. Patrick couldn't figure out why Brenda's parents bought a condo in a building filled with old people and a few Orthodox couples whose kids had just moved out. Her dad had hinted that he got a deal, but it was probably the only place he could afford. The umbrellaed tables were occupied by the usual groups of old people playing euchre and a game that might have been bridge. A few of the card players were concentration camp survivors; even on the hottest days they wore long sleeves and bracelets to conceal tattooed wrists.

At the first table, an old lady in a loose-fitting shirt that looked as if it had been sewn from rejected floral-pattern samples was picking up her cards. She was fidgety, prey to tics, and drew wavy patterns in the air with her bony hands and bangles. An internal clock set her eyes sweeping the poolside at two-minute intervals. It was true, he had timed her: every couple of minutes her eyes made their rounds, searchlights hunting down loose links in the fence or stopping for a quick inspection of Patrick's blue eyes and light hair as he sat playing cards with Brenda.

Brenda was waiting for him at their usual table, her chair almost pushed against the fence. Behind the fence the grass wall of the highway embankment rose up like the base of an ancient earth mound whose shape — a snake or a man or a raven — was only visible from high in the air. But even dwarfed by the embankment and the sun umbrella, Brenda's sun hat looked unnaturally large, as if it were drawn to a slightly larger scale than the surrounding scene. The hat must belong to her mother. It wouldn't have taken Brenda more than five seconds to find her own hat, the nice white one that showed off her cheekbones, and put it on. She could have tried a little harder to look good, instead of always trailing some reminder of her parents' dreary apartment, like a little girl returning from the bathroom with a toilet-paper tail. It was like she did it on purpose, like she didn't want to be as beautiful as nature had intended her to be. He could hear himself saying these cruel things. He had to stop. Now, at the end of things, he was finally going to play by the rules — no accusations, no insults, nothing to make her feel that the breakup was her fault.

Patrick sat down across from Brenda and then stood up so quickly that someone watching would have thought that his chair was electrically charged. Brenda smiled and waited for him to launch into one of his elaborate anecdotes, perhaps about a man who had sat on a piece of gum on the long bus ride up Bathurst. But the sun had ironed Patrick's black jeans to his thighs. He couldn't wear them for another second. He began to strip down to the cut-off track pants he wore under his jeans, Brenda still waiting for the anecdote to begin. The hat drooped in folds around her face, as if the material were melting in the heat, and when she saw his expression as he folded his jeans she flicked one of the folds with her finger and rolled her eyes, pre-empting whatever mean thing he was going to say about the hat. She said she wanted to play euchre.

Patrick sat down again and folded his arms across his stomach. He tried to mentally locate the spot that actors were trained to project their voices from — the diaphragm. If he forced himself to speak from that spot then all of this would be more like a play. He would tell her that they had to break up, she would cry, he would exit through a fake door. On the embankment behind the fence two paths had been beaten down in the long grass. The grass was slicked in one direction as if it had been carefully combed and gelled for a party. A bunch of people must have climbed the embankment to spray-paint their names on the noise-reduction wall and then slid down the grass to the fence. It was probably a bunch of kids using the embankment as a place to drink and fool around. He imagined drunken teenagers sliding down the embankment on strips of cardboard, jerked into sudden heaps at the base of the high fence, laughing and showing off their scrapes and bruises and then sliding down the hill again, all the while hoping to be caught at their game by some bitter adult too old to hop the fence and kick their asses.

Patrick didn't want to play cards. He should tell Brenda that he didn't want to play but she was already shuffling her favourite deck of cards. She was always telling him they were her favourite deck but never told him why. The deck wasn't old. It hadn't been passed down to her by a scandalous relative trailing the perfumes of Old World sensuality and intrigue. She hadn't taught him any new games either. Why hadn't she ever asked one of the old people to teach them that game that was like bridge? Maybe it was bridge they were playing. Patrick would never find out now. He wanted to tear that hat off Brenda's head and throw it over the fence, where the teenagers would make fun of it when they were drunk.

Brenda dealt the cards. She won the first three hands, but the games were close. Even at the end of everything Patrick still hated losing. He knew what Brenda wanted to ask: was he going to invite her out to the Coast? The question of their future together had been sitting between them like a fat chaperone since he'd told her he wanted to move to Vancouver Island to work at a restaurant owned by Steve's uncle. Brenda was starting her English degree at U of T in the fall, but she'd started hinting about transferring her first-year credits to Victoria in a year. She also started reminding Patrick that he had promised himself to start working on his B.A. soon. The longer he kept his silence on the question the clearer a vision of their shared future took hold of Brenda's imagination.

Patrick forced himself to lose the next few hands. When Brenda tried to start a conversation he answered with mono-syllables and grunts. He was demonstrating his unhappiness so that when she looked back on this afternoon she would know that he had arrived at the pool unhappy. He didn't want her to blame their breakup on the eruption of one of their ongoing arguments. When she was up nine points to one he told her he didn't want to play anymore.

"But we're almost finished," she said.

"So, I don't want to play."

Her mouth opened. Patrick willed her to stand up to him, to start a fight that would lead to ultimatums and insults. He wanted to feel the full wash of her shame and anger. She never got mad at him. It was a point of pride for her to never get angry. That was how she won arguments. Brenda began fidgeting with the cards, her expression veiled by the hat. The old lady with the searchlight eyes was watching them from across the pool. The old lady was staring at him, her black eyes seeming to retract deeper into their sockets, as if in the camps her eyeballs had evolved this defensive function to increase their range of movement. Patrick, singled out and powerful, felt himself transformed into a man to be feared, a conqueror amidst a subject people, before he plunged into shame remembering the source of this unearned power. These people are all fucking paranoid, Patrick thought. You couldn't blame them — they were Jews, people were always finding excuses to kill them. All they'd been through, even the ones who weren't in the camps, just to sit beside this pool playing cards and waiting to die. They should be travelling the world, telling their stories, and teaching people to be good to each other or at least not to kill each other.

There was another survivor playing at the old woman's table, an old man who wore short sleeves and the top three buttons of his cotton shirt open as if he were just another guy enjoying his retirement. He had been a jeweller and watchmaker, and now fixed appliances free of charge for his fellow tenants. He often talked about his children and grandchildren with chastising affection, and the spare, thoughtful way he dealt the cards reminded Patrick of the priest who prepared the Eucharist feast at the church his family joined the year his dad gave up drinking. Steve would have described the old Jewish guy as "very Zen," a man who, after being stripped of his worldly illusions in the camps with the speed of a gang rape, had found his way out of blame and hatred to acceptance and emptiness.

In Patrick's version of things the old man had just learned

to hide from his past. The old man had carefully formulated a set of routines and stock phrases to get through the day without thinking about the camps, his personal calendar a clockwork where the second and hour hands never met. According to Brenda, the old man played the same six lottery numbers every week, a sequence he had chosen by combining the digits tattooed on his wrist.

Patrick motioned toward the old man as Brenda swept up the cards. "What would happen if that old guy actually won the lottery?"

"He'd probably divide the money amongst his kids and their kids."

"Then I bet he'd jump off the roof." Patrick only half believed this, but some part of him, a hidden entity who occasionally hijacked his thoughts, not only wanted it to be true but wanted to be there when the old man finally lost all hope and killed himself.

"Didn't you sleep well last night?" she asked him.

"What's that got to do with it?"

"You look tired, that's all."

"You know, you don't have to reduce all my emotions and my, my *ideas* to symptoms of illness." She wasn't really doing this, but she also wasn't saying what she really meant, which was worse somehow.

"That's not what I was doing."

"Yes you were."

"You don't have to yell."

"I barely raised my voice. What is this, the fucking House of Usher? I just don't feel like playing cards, you don't have to read into it."

She raised her fingertips from the table in a fan, sign language for "fine, whatever."

He put his face within slapping range. He had it coming. He treated her like shit — she had to see that. He would have cancelled his trip to the Coast for Amy but he wouldn't even ask Brenda to come for a visit.

"I ran into Amy Stern on the way here," he said.

Brenda bowed her head a little more, drawing the veil of hat fringes over her expression again. "How is she?"

"I think her dad is thinking of moving the family back to Israel. At least for a year. He's been offered a job at a university there. He's very smart," he said. "Did you know that he was the prof who had his monkeys stolen? It was in the papers." The last part wasn't true, but the knowledge that Brenda could easily find him out made Patrick feel like he was suffering from vertigo. The tabletop where his hands rested was a hundred feet below him.

"I didn't hear about it."

"Well, it was him," he said. "A bunch of these animal rights people let his monkeys go. And when they caught them he didn't even punish them." This was the important point — the even-handed, paternal way Amy's father handled the situation. "He could have had them put away for years."

"The monkeys?"

"What?"

"Why would he put the monkeys away for years?"

"He wouldn't put the monkeys away," he said. "They just left their cages to look for food."

"I thought you meant that he could have had the monkeys put away for years, which is weird because the monkeys are already in cages."

"No, the animal rights people," he said, delivering the final lines in what he realized was one of Brenda's long, punchlineless jokes. "They got caught and he didn't press charges. I think he probably sympathizes with their point of view — the activists, not the fucking monkeys. Anyways, I don't think Amy wants to go to Israel."

"She'd probably have to join the army," Brenda said.

"I think she wants to," he said.

"She'll be old enough next year, won't she?" Her tone implied that not only had she long suspected his feelings for Amy but she had already convicted him for crimes of emotional foolishness. Again he wished she would get angry. She certainly didn't seem surprised. Still looking down at the cards, she slid the Queen of Spades over the Queen of Hearts, dramatizing the victory of darkness over light, lust over true love, then laid her hand palm-up to highlight the gesture's obvious symbolism.

See what I mean, he was saying in his head, his lips barely keeping pace with the words, *she never says what she's thinking*. He sat back in his chair and looked up at the embankment, arguing with her in his mind, scoring points at her expense. She was manipulative. She brought this on herself by not confronting him. If you're going to let people walk all over you then you can't complain about what they do to you. When his fury subsided Patrick explained to this phantom Brenda that he was all wrong for her. He never knew the right things to say to her to make her happy. She thought that because she knew so much about him that he must know at least as much about her. She couldn't be more wrong. He was stupid that way, he could admit it. Even after going out with her for almost two years he had no idea what she was thinking at any given moment. He couldn't imagine what she acted like when he wasn't with her. Conversations and nightly phone calls provided him with the external details — what she ate for dinner, how her drawings were coming along, what she and Esther and Laurie talked about at the bagel shop — but he couldn't connect them into a picture of a living person. What did she feel? Why did she do one thing and not another? How did her voice and gestures change when she was away from him?

Patrick felt better explaining this to Brenda in his mind. They really weren't right for each other. She needed a more sensitive man, he needed a blunter woman. It was out of their hands. He felt a wave of possessive affection for her. He wanted her to be happy. He reached across the table and cupped his hand over hers. "I think I just need to go for a swim," he said. "I'm fucking dying in this heat." She asked if he wanted a towel and he told her not to worry, that he'd dry off in the sun. He was trying to tell her that his mood would improve with a swim, but she settled back into her chair, hiding under her sun hat.

The only other people in the pool were an old couple he didn't recognize who were treading water just deep enough to drown them if they stopped paddling. The water was always warm but he tested it with his toes, afraid that the pool might have been drained and refilled before the weekend. Patrick was afraid of cold water, or any sudden change to his metabolism. He was ashamed of this fear. He would practise swimming in cold water out on the Coast. He had to get tougher. He had to untangle his life and become strong again. He could remember a time when he was stronger, when his thoughts and feelings flowed as bright and strong as scenes unfolding in a good movie. He dived into the water and his body was stripped of the layer of heat and sweat as quickly as a Band-Aid being torn from his skin. He came up and shook his head and after taking a deep breath swam to the bottom of the pool. He touched the con-crete and turned onto his back, paddling his arms and legs to stay on the bottom. The water tried to push him up so he increased his body weight by expelling some of the air from his lungs. He was buried under tons of water but he had to work like a bastard to hold his position at the bottom. Patrick opened his eyes. The sun, a big fried egg of light, sizzled and spat sparks in the sky above him. Then the sky was rent by a cannonball as the old jeweller, hugging his knees to his chest, dragging the tattered sun in his wake, sank halfway to the bottom of the pool before spreading his bubbled wings and taking flight.

Stepping into the elevator with Brenda, pressing the button for the 17th floor, Patrick rehearsed the future. He and Brenda would take the elevator to the top floor, then the short flight of stairs to the roof. On the roof of the building, Brenda would be surprised when he didn't light a joint or make a pass at her —— he usually only asked her to go up to the roof to do things he couldn't do by the pool or in her bedroom. Patrick would begin the speech that he had been practising for days, telling her that it was time for them to part. Brenda would look him in the eyes as he spoke and this time he would not look away. She would listen to his speech, consider his points, and in a tearful moment of revelation admit that he was right, that things really were over between them.

Patrick replayed this fantasy as the elevator began to rise. His heart was running away from him — his heart had jumped from its throne and was running around his chest pounding at the walls. Brenda looked at him in a friendly, forgiving way. She didn't suspect anything. She was waiting for his mood to pass. He was always in a mood — he hated that about himself. It was one of the things he was going to change. He was going to get stronger.

In the fantasy he said goodbye to Brenda. What if a blackout hit the neighbourhood after he said goodbye? They would be forced to take the stairs down to Brenda's apartment on the ninth floor where her parents would be worrying about her, listening for details about the blackout on the battery-powered radio they kept in a drawer in the kitchen. They would pull Brenda into the apartment and ask Patrick in but he would say he had to get home. There would be no scene when he said goodbye to Brenda for the final time. Then he would head back to the staircase, passing between apartment doors maniacally opening and closing, the hallway a row of life-size cuckoo clocks chiming, "Where are the lights, where are the lights?" On the way down the stairs Patrick would hear a noise, the low moaning of a woman in terrible pain. He would race through the shadows, through the patches of black between the emergency lights. On the third floor landing Patrick would find the old woman with the searchlight eyes sprawled, propped against the wall, holding her hand over her right hip. She would have fallen, her hip bone popped with a sound like an old tree knot splintering in a fire. The woman would look up at Patrick as he came down to her from the shadowed stairs. He'd emerge from the darkness into the emergency light, and in his pale skin and blue eyes she would see a shadow of the young Pole who turned her and her sisters into the ss for an extra ration of cabbage and bitter chocolate. In his black jeans and T-shirt, see the uniform of the ss officer who pulled her sister out of the line just to scar her face with a cigarette. But the old woman would be too pain-drugged to fight as Patrick carefully lifted her off the floor. Cradling her shattered hip, Patrick would carry the old woman up four flights of stairs to her tidy apartment. In the fading light from the windows the sepia-tinted photos of dead relatives would blend into the walls like water stains. He would lay the old woman on the couch and phone the ambulance. He would get the old woman a drink, some aspirin, and an ice pack, and as she lay there he would tell her stories to take her mind off the pain. He would tell her about his grandparents' life in the old Toronto Catholic ghetto, which was not a ghetto like Warsaw, he knows, but there was suffering there, too. The old woman would understand. She would tell him that people are people, and that's not usually a good thing. People do terrible things to each other, the old woman would explain, though by now she would know that Patrick understood this painful truth, and that in spite of the years and miles and suffering between them he is a kindred soul. Nothing he would tell the old woman would shock her — a lifetime of his sins wouldn't match an hour of the crimes she had seen. In the fantasy he began to tell the woman all the bad things he had done to people. He admitted that he had been cruel to Brenda. He should have done everything differently from the start, he should have loved Brenda more. But it was too late now. The bones he had broken in their relationship had set crooked and stiff. He and Brenda could not move forward.

When the elevator reached the top floor Patrick stepped into the hallway and began walking toward the staircase. He wanted more time alone with his fantasy. He was telling the old woman how he wished he could change things. The old woman took his hand. She told him not to worry about what he had done in the past. She could see that he was sorry. All he could do now was to change the future.

Patrick reached the door to the staircase. Brenda was walking down the centre of the hallway. The receding lines of the hallway and the repetitive pattern on the carpet seemed to levitate her body above the floor. She was floating toward him. Her face was composed. She either had no idea what was about to happen or she didn't believe that he could go through with his plan. The miracle of her innocence bore her above the floor like a queen in her litter.

Patrick ran up the stairs to the roof and opened the heavy door. The sky was huge. The sky was everywhere. He heard Brenda walk onto the roof behind him. She was leaning against the wall of the small out-building that housed the elevator shaft. She was waiting for him to do something. She looked tired but didn't want to show it. How many times had he brought that expression to her face? Her face was going to freeze that way if he didn't do something. Patrick walked over to Brenda and rested his hands on her shoulders and kissed her on the mouth. The future was telling him to do this, to kiss her more passionately than he ever had before. He was stepping out of his own glorious future to give her a taste of the man he would be some day and to show her the woman she could be. He kissed her mouth and neck. He nuzzled her with his nose, gently mocking her shyness, and she rose up out of her habits and grabbed the back of his neck and laid a trail of kisses from his mouth to his earlobe, which she bit and tongued until he had to moan, surprised.

They found each other's soft spots and worked them over gently, and she surprised him again by undoing his pants without prompting. Her body was moving with his. They were finally going someplace together, neither of them leading the other. This is how it should have always been. She took his half-hard cock out of his pants and began to knead his flesh. He hated the way she jerked him off, with two fingers and a thumb, as if she were trying to remold his cock instead of honouring the simple geometry finding form in her hand. He clamped her hand into a tube and holding the tube started a simple rhythm she could follow.

"Don't you like it?" she asked.

She'd never learned to handle his cock, and he'd never told her how to. If she were a stronger person, he could have cracked a joke about the quality of her hand jobs, how he could do what she was doing but better. Even a strong girl would be hurt by such a taunt, but a strong girl would rise to the challenge and ask him to demonstrate his preferred technique. I'm sure you've had lots of practice, this strong girl would joke, putting him in his place.

It was too late to tell Brenda now. She'd think he'd been lying all those times he told her how good she was in bed. He hadn't been lying, not really. He had enjoyed himself. Brenda lifted up his shirt and began to kiss his stomach. "No, no," he said, almost meaning it, offering the words as evidence of a warning as she pulled down his pants to his knees. She took him in her mouth and he leaned back against the wall and closed his eyes. The sound of the traffic on the highway far below them was a tide. Everything was airy now, especially Brenda's hair in his hands. Everything was lighter, except for his groin, which felt encircled by a metal ring, a moment of radiance recorded in soft iron. His thighs were limp. He had to lock his knees like the legs of a folding table to stop from falling forward. He was rising up into the sky and the tides. He was passing over time and space to the future. Everything was clear — sky and mountains, the ocean and old trees and a hot bowl of noodles. He was rising.

When he came the building beneath him dropped a foot, an elevator correcting itself after overleaping its floor. His knees buckled. He grabbed Brenda's shoulders to stop from toppling over her. He fell against her again as his legs, already wobbled by orgasm, were caught in mid-stride by his dropped pants. There was nothing to do but surrender to the low comedy. He started laughing as Brenda helped him to stand up straight. He was surprised and relieved when Brenda stood up laughing. He buried his face in her hair and moaned.

"I'm sooooo weak."

"We'll bring up some crutches or leg braces for you next time," she said.

"That's funny," he said. He got her into a playful head-lock and kissed the top of her head, remembering that she could be funny when she wanted to be. "Why don't you make more jokes?" he asked.

"You don't give me a chance."

"What? Christ, I'm a walking punchline-vending machine. How many times have I fed you a perfect line at a party? All the times I've said something so stupid." He was enjoying the smell of her scalp, her cool neck. The pressure that he hadn't known was there was gone from his chest. It would build again. Right now, though, he was at peace. This was the last time he would see Brenda for a long time. Nothing he said could be used against him in future arguments, there was nothing he could use against her. For the first time since they'd met they were free of the picture that each of them had built of the other. He wanted to explain that to her.

"All the times I've set you up for a punchline," he said. "You could have creamed me a hundred times."

"I never want to make you look like a fool."

"As if I ever needed help, eh?"

"That's not it, you know that."

He did know what she meant, though he couldn't put it into words. She was telling him something about love. He tried to find his way back to the moments before the orgasm when everything had been so clear, but it was like trying to climb a ladder made out of mist.

"Do you think I'm an idiot?" he asked, knowing that she wouldn't answer. Her silence was her way of pushing him to find his own answer. She was looking up at him. The tired expression on her face was set against his stupidity. He had to try to understand her just this one time.

"I like it when you make fun of me," he said.

"I don't."

"But I never make fun of you."

"No, silly, I mean that I don't like making fun of *you*. Well, sometimes I do, but not usually."

He tried to understand. She was telling him that she had

a reason for saving up her jokes for special moments, like when her lover's knees buckled during orgasm. She didn't make jokes about Patrick when other people were around — that would be too easy. Was that what she was telling him? He felt himself blush. She was still holding his cock so he squeezed her hand and let out an outraged cry of pain. "Not so hard!" He did it again. "Ow!" Her face went slack, then she laughed and nodded in mock disgust.

"How come you never look at me like you're really looking at me?" he asked. "It's like you're looking through me — no, like you're looking at something inside me."

"I am," she said.

"What are you looking at?"

"I wish you could see yourself when you're asleep."

"Me too," he said. "That would mean I could leave my body."

She looked away from him. She thought he was joking, but he was admitting something very painful: the idea of being able to leave his body at will and roam the world invisible and untouchable was one of his oldest fantasies.

"It's funny," she said. "When you're asleep you look like a little boy who's thinking the thoughts of a very old man."

He leaned into her again. "My grandmother said that she knew right away that I had an *old soul*, that I had been here before."

"You probably have," she said, her tone not signalling whether she thought that this was a good thing or not.

"*You* haven't," he said.

"God, I know." She shook her head. "This is all new to me."

He stroked her hair. He was going to tell her — any second now. The day was finally starting to cool down. He was going to tell her.

MY GOD, RICHARD IS BEAUTIFUL

Theresa and Paul get off knowing this can't go further than sex. Theresa is also Richard's girlfriend, which should make sex with Paul a crime. Paul looks at Theresa's naked body for proof of Richard's claim, a booby-trapped mole that triggered will bring Richard rushing into the room to charge Paul with crimes of betrayed friendship. Paul prods her stomach and ribs, then pretends to pinch off little rolls of skin as if she's an uncooked pastry, some loaf stuffed with clotted cream baked for a Saint's day. When he cups her breast and makes to kiss the protruding nipple she pushes his hand away and says, "Dirty fucker," and they laugh.

"Just because you fucked me doesn't mean you can touch my breasts."

"I'll never be affectionate again," he says.

Theresa doesn't seem to feel guilty about fucking Paul. She enjoys sex more than any woman he's ever been with. She gives herself over to pornography-free sex for hours — no lingerie or leather, she doesn't call him Daddy or say *my pussy* or tell him how big and hard he is. Paul wonders if she is exempted from guilt through some loophole claimable only by lovers in the highest sexual income bracket, which would make Paul her tax shelter, some offshore account in Bermuda where she launders her excess lust.

He closes his eyes and he can see the two of them fucking

again. Theresa arching her head back, wringing the little pillow beneath her like a wet face cloth. Paul pinning her arms and Theresa giving him a look that says, "I could free myself if I wanted." Finally there's the picture of her bedroom window, a bright white box hanging in space before orgasm squeezed his eyes shut.

Paul loves the way she rests her cigarette on her belly, the filter wedged into the island of her cupped hand, a little lighthouse on a calm, foggy sea. The smoke spirals up in long beanstalks that decompose and hang in the humidity over the bed.

"Do you know what book I had my mom read to me every night?" he asks her. "Jack and the Beanstalk."

"Why?"

"I don't know. I don't even remember her reading it to me, but she told me I demanded it every night. I brought it up to be poignant."

"You mean, intimate."

"We should get married."

"We don't have to."

"I'm tired of being your mistress."

"No you're not."

Theresa giggles and takes a long drag and blows a line of smoke across his belly and down into his pubic hair. He wishes she would kiss his belly and chest, even rest a hand there. She always bites and kisses his face and neck, leaving patches of spasming skin, but there is a long stretch between his Adam's apple and belly button that her lips barely graze on route to the more important business of raising sex. Couldn't she just kiss his stomach? That's part of it — *that's what you do.* It's like a story and she skips the middle chapters to get to the big battle scene at the end. He calls her before his mind and tells her that now she's the one being mean.

He hints again that they should get serious and she

answers so quickly that she must have been expecting the offer. "No way," she says. "I know I'm not your first choice. That's fine if you want to fuck me, but not if you want me to be your girlfriend." Meaning she is Richard's first choice, which is true.

Paul has a crush on a waitress at Lee's, and if it came down to a choice between her and Theresa he'd pick the waitress. Paul doesn't know why, but he has to sleep with the waitress. She makes him feel weak and useless when she serves him a drink and doesn't laugh at his jokes. He has to make the waitress laugh.

Richard doesn't want anyone but Theresa. If Paul was as good-looking as Richard he would fuck a different woman every night until he'd tried every flavour and combination of flavours he could imagine. But Richard has never gone on a spree. One woman at a time — and not always the prettiest. There's no explaining it. Paul thinks about the big room in Richard's basement, where Richard has set up his own version of a living room and kitchen. There are a couple of 1960s' easy chairs, Richard's portable stereo, a coffee table donated by Paul, a hot plate to make tea and grilled-cheese sandwiches. Paul and Richard and Gary used to hang out there after school to smoke a joint and listen to records and boil water for an endless pot of steadily weakening tea. Richard called those afternoons "playing house," the loud punk music and joints and outdated furniture a big "fuck you" to his parents' living room upstairs. Paul is beginning to drift off. He sees Gary pretending to masturbate on Richard's Sid Vicious poster and Richard pretending not to care. He sees Richard stack three grilled-cheese sandwiches and somehow get his mouth around the whole stack. He sees the brown teapot bow again and again. Richard says "playing house," only it sounds like "praying house." Richard has a beautiful mouth.

Theresa nudges Paul awake as she lights another cigarette. Paul says "Aida" and they start laughing. Aida lives in a condo on Bay Street that her parents bought her. She's a rich girl who studies something left-wing at York. Theresa is from the wrong side of the tracks, so everything she says waves a flag of authenticity in Aida's face. Aida lets Theresa crash in the spare bedroom when she comes downtown to party. It's an empty room with a carpet thicker than a futon, but Theresa is not allowed to fuck anyone in there. That would be taking advantage of Aida's *stuff*. But the other night after Aida went to bed, Paul and Theresa went into the spare room and started fooling around. It was the first time they'd touched each other since Theresa starting dating Richard last summer.

"I fucked Aida, eh," Paul says.

"You *didn't*," she says, hoping he did.

"I did."

"Oh. My. God. You're a pig!"

"You told me to!"

"I did not."

He realizes that he's been saving this story for the right moment. "Me and you were starting to fool around at Aida's and then you said, 'I can't do it anymore, I'm just too drunk.'" Paul's imitation of Theresa consists of lowering his voice, though hers is much higher than his. "So I grabbed my hard-on and said, 'What am I going to with this?' and you said, 'If it's green, see a doctor!'"

"I did?" Theresa's almost in tears. If Paul had a kid sister he would have tried to make her laugh like this.

"You did, so I said, 'What am I going to do with this *right now*? I can't sleep on it, it'll break.' And you said, 'Go fuck Aida.'"

"No!" Her mouth freezes on the "o."

"You told me to go fuck Aida — so I did."

"You fucked her!"

"Sure."

Theresa actually shrieks. "How was it?"

"Terrible, of course." Though it wasn't bad at all. He'd walked into Aida's room and found her watching Looney Tunes on the big TV at the end of her bed. They smoked a joint. Aida began explaining that Bugs Bunny was a trickster figure appropriated by white American cartoon directors, so Paul called her a wannabe French intellectual. She said that he was the worst kind of prole — a prole with half a brain. He said that the Roadrunner was the American Dream and Coyote an immigrant labourer. Aida called him an idiot. He laughed and said, "Let's take a bath."

Later he knelt above Aida on her big decadent bed and rubbed his cock on her body. Her skin was honey golden, his pale arm a seam of quartz opening up in her golden belly. One light was on. The bedroom was filled with tasteful things her parents had bought her — art and books and good furniture. Aida held her body in pornographic poses, playing with her nipples, looking him in the eye through a curtain of hair that she flicked aside when she went down on him. She made a game out of silence, as if a single noise would bring the palace guards rushing in with their castration shears. The more she enjoyed the sex the harder she fought for silence, even gritting her teeth when she came and putting her fingers over his mouth when he did. She said that next time it would be his turn to "strike some pretty poses." He said, "Yes, mistress."

They were joking, but they weren't.

Theresa lights another cigarette. "So you fucked her and came back to bed with me?"

"Even I couldn't do something that scummy. I came back

to you before you woke up because she went out to break-fast with Bill."

"Bill came over?" Theresa can't believe how much she missed. "And she didn't invite you to eat?"

"She left an opening, but she knows I'm broke 'til my next cheque." Aida still had that over him. When she first came on the scene she told Theresa and Richard not to invite Paul to her parties. Aida had it in for Paul, no one could figure out why. His friends offered to boycott her parties, but Paul said no, go without him, he'd make Aida invite him one day. She even spread rumours about Paul, how he used Richard for his good looks and drug connections.

Then one night an old queer Paul had met in the liquor store invited him to what turned out to be a swingers' party. Paul had brought Theresa and her sister Lisa. After a few drinks and literary conversation, people started making out and taking off their clothes. Theresa and Lisa were grossed out and finally pulled Paul out of there when the old queer started setting up a video camera. Then Theresa said that Aida was having a party, why not go there and see if she had the guts to kick Paul out. They'd all done some coke at the party. They wanted something to happen. Paul said, "Fuck yeah!" They just walked into the middle of Aida's party and Paul yelled, "Hey, who wants to be in a fucking porno film? I know where they're shooting one right now." That got everyone's attention. They all wanted to hear about the old swinger's party. "My God," Paul shouted, "half the cast of Laugh-In was there!" Everybody laughed. Aida had to let him stay.

"God, she's cheap," Theresa says.

"And she's a bad lay."

Paul wonders why he's lying, or half lying, to Theresa. The way Aida bit her lip when he was fucking her. Sex with her was a big, dirty put-on, but he was going to go back to her bed, he might as well admit it. He would go back until Aida lost her power over him. Theresa would mock him for fucking Aida again, but Theresa has her own weaknesses — she's going out with Richard, for God's sake.

"Poor Aida." Theresa says this with real sympathy. Because she sees everything clearer than Paul, Theresa forgives easier. "She tries to be cool, she really tries. You know her and Lisa stole a bunch of halibut fillets, eh, from Bill's freezer at that party a couple of weeks ago."

"Halibut? *Halibut*." That's the funniest thing Paul has ever heard — why not cod?

"That's just mean," Theresa says. "Of course I ate three of them — they were delicious. Aida's so fucking mean to Bill — she gets off on it. At least Lisa has an excuse to be mean." When she was sixteen Theresa went to live with an aunt in Hamilton, leaving Lisa with their alcoholic mother, who wouldn't let both daughters move away from her. Thinking about Lisa, Theresa says what she always says: "I never should have left her with that crazy bitch."

Paul could console Theresa by reminding her that she was only sixteen at the time. He could say that it's human nature to protect yourself, and that people who've been through what they've been through only survive by making terrible sacrifices. But he can't share this wisdom with her — it would mean nothing coming from a fellow sufferer. He doesn't know why. Only a man who hasn't suffered what they have suffered will be able to comfort her. Paul doesn't know who this man is — he is hidden out there in the world waiting to liberate Theresa. This man is quiet, patient, whole, maybe a little stupid. Kind of like Richard, but Richard is a rehearsal for the real man.

The whole set-up is sad. But Paul wouldn't have it any other way, because if there's a man out there for Theresa then there must be a woman for him, too. He knows the house this woman grew up in — tasteful and old and cared for by doting, slightly decadent parents. Paul will marry this woman some day. She worries about Paul. She looks for solutions to his problems. She wants him to tackle his fears, which lie in his chest like a den of snakes he's afraid to wake. She comes to him after sex and lays her head on his chest to listen to the sound of all his terrible fears, lying in him like snakes. Then she begins to sing, quietly calling out his fears, her voice reaching in to untangle and pull the snakes from their nest one at a time. With her soft, strong hands she holds the snakes in the air, and one by one she names them — "This is what your daddy did to you," "This is what your mommy didn't do to you." She soothes the snakes — it turns out that they're afraid, too — stroking their heads until they drop limp, and then she lays them out on the bed in rows. The snakes are tapered and strong and shimmer with metallic colour, lined up on the clean white sheet like ornamental weapons. She drains their venom into a golden cup and he swallows the poison in one gulp. The next morning he wakes up the strongest, wisest man in the world, ready to sire her children, who will know nothing of his past but that their daddy has been in the fire and was burned clean and that he would die to protect them.

Paul likes the word *sire*. No one uses it anymore.

Paul can hear the angry rush-hour traffic down on the expressway, the drivers judging all the young lovers who have fucked the afternoon away. Paul's welfare cheque is due in three days, and he makes a bit of money on the side working the door at a booze can two nights a week. He is in bed with his friend's girlfriend and soon they will eat Kraft Dinner and joke about how broke they are and then go downtown and get drinks bought for them. And a girl in the

bar will want to go to bed with him, and at least six boys —
and a couple of girls — will fall in love with Theresa.

Paul doesn't want to be in this heat anymore. He's pressed
like a leaf between layers of humidity and cigarette smoke.
Theresa is probably asleep. Her body can pass into sleep
without a signal. There is no winding down, no process, she
just rests her head on the nearest shoulder-shaped surface
and the bright lights behind her eyes go out in a flutter.

Theresa isn't asleep. She lights a cigarette and tells Paul
that Lisa called earlier. Where was he when she called? He
hasn't left the apartment since they woke up at about noon.
He should have at least heard the phone ring, or heard
Theresa talking in the living room. He tries to lure the
memory by combining, in his imagination, the sound of a
phone ringing and the visual of Theresa jumping off the bed
naked, which she had done an hour ago to put the kettle on.
He makes Theresa say, "Hello, hello, Lisa, where the fuck
were you?" but still, he has no memory of her answering the
phone. He's been losing memories lately — they disappear
like volcanic islands exploding and sinking behind him as he
is pulled forward in time. He'd gotten a rash last summer:
what if it was syphilis and he's going crazy now?

"I thought we were going to look for her again tonight,"
he says, as if Theresa has deliberately spoiled their plans.

"Well, we don't have to. She's staying at Jerry's."

"That fucking old creep at The 360?"

"He's all right when he's buying you beer."

"He's got date-rapist written all over him. He's Mr.
December on the date-rape calendar."

"And you're Mr. June."

"Come on."

"Okay, you're on a different calendar."

"Just, you should have told me she called."

"You were worried?"

"Fuck off."

"*Were* you worried?"

"She's your sister."

"Exactly." This is Theresa's way of telling him that she knows he's up to something with Lisa. Paul isn't even sure what he's up to. He's flirted with Lisa a few times — he's considered her, of course. Lisa is like Theresa in all the important ways. She never talks about the future. She loves her body, she drinks and eats like a man — so many of the women Paul's slept with seem ashamed of eating in front of their lovers.

Lisa is a lot like Theresa, but something sets her apart. A second skin, of sadness or something, slows her movements even at the wildest parties. She's always alone. In the deepest forests a clearing would still surround her.

"I think she's got a crush on me," he says, hopefully.

"Fucking right she does. Don't you lay a hand on her."

"She's better off with Jerry, eh."

"And she can't know about us." Theresa is looking at Paul. She lights another cigarette. "Especially if you do sleep with her."

Theresa has backed down from her first prohibition, a retreat that strengthens her second prohibition while downgrading the first to a warning to proceed cautiously. Now that he knows that he will sleep with Lisa, and that something good will come out of it, he wants to begin things with her honestly. He's not a liar, he can say that much. "She's gotta know we've slept together, at least last summer."

"She doesn't." Theresa says. "She'd never forgive me."

"But you're not doing anything wrong. To her."

"Don't pull this *priest* shit on me."

The word priest scares him. Theresa has chosen it so unselfconsciously, as if she or someone else, maybe even a whole room full of people, have described him as a priest before. This has been happening to Paul all summer — the sudden feeling that his friends and enemies know a humiliating truth about him, followed by the revelation that if this is true they must all be humouring his ignorance, probably because they think he is too weak to handle the truth.

Paul needs Theresa to be loyal to him right now. He needs some of the pity and love she must lavish on Richard, and he knows he won't get it. Somewhere along the way Paul and Theresa agreed to be tough on each other. But last night, for a little while, he was sure that he was in love with her. They'd been downtown looking for Lisa, whom Theresa hadn't seen since the party at Aida's on the weekend. They were holding hands on Harbord, on their way from Lee's to The 360, and Theresa began telling him about something terrible that her dad used to do when he was drunk. She was picking up the thread of a conversation they'd dropped who knew how many days earlier. They'd been out somewhere trading funny stories about their drunken fathers when they'd gotten interrupted. It all came back to him in a second, as if the time between conversations had just been a pause for breath. Thinking of this wonderful power Theresa had over his memory, Paul squeezed her hand, and she squeezed back.

Paul rolls over and rests his hand on Theresa's arm, then inches his hand down to hers. "When is Richard coming back?"

"Monday."

Richard has been up at his family cottage for over a week helping his stepfather shingle the roof.

"Are you going to go over to his place when he gets back?" Paul asks.

"Why wouldn't I?"

Paul wonders if she'll tell Richard about them. She won't. If Paul asked her she would just say that Richard doesn't need to know. This has nothing to do with Richard.

"What am I going to do with this?" Paul asks.

"If it's green, see a doctor. Don't call me."

"Richard," he says. He misses Richard. He knows what everyone says about Richard behind his back, but he'd never tell Richard. Paul would never hurt Richard.

Theresa says, "Richard," his name earing a long drag on her cigarette. "His wrist is limp but his dick is hard." She sits up. "*Oh my God*, did that just come out of my mouth? I sound like my mother." She laughs and lies back down. "My God, Richard is beautiful. I mean, it's a gift."

"A gift from the gods," Paul says, imagining a long hall of marble statues of beautiful boys in classical poses — reclining, listening attentively, cocking an arm, being admired. Women often give Paul a second look, but he has to earn the third. Women can't stop looking at Richard. His beauty is as biologically indisputable as a third nipple.

Theresa rolls on her side and wipes a leech of hair from Paul's forehead, all motherly. "It's weird with Richard, you know," she says. "He knows he's good-looking, but he doesn't own his good looks. He hasn't worked for them. But that's not what I mean."

Paul doesn't like where this is going. He wouldn't have guessed that Richard's looks had any real power over Theresa. He should have known better. He and Theresa always lust after the same kind of beauty — lovers with big eyes and lips and cheekbones and pale smooth skin, half-amphibians that look as if they gestated in their mother's wombs until puberty.

"He reminds me of a rare butterfly pinned in some collector's glass box," Paul says. "But he's the collector and the butterfly at the same time."

"My God, he's beautiful. It kind of makes me sick. Really, like I get nauseated looking at him for too long. It's like eating too much dessert." She laughs and hugs Paul as if he's just given her a present.

"He looks like his own drawings," Paul says.

"That's it!"

They both must be picturing Richard's sketch pad, its stylized doodles of faces ennobled by high cheekbones and cruel lips, feline eyes looking out at withered trees and low hills, because they groan and laugh. Paul takes Theresa into his arms again but it's too hot in the room. He starts to kiss her neck and she asks what time it is and lights another cigarette. He wishes he smoked.

Paul catalogues everything in the bedroom. A particle-board dresser with a couple of missing drawer handles topped with a mirror shaped like a cartoon crown. A queen-size bed the sisters share. A little rickety table beside the bed. This is all connected to the way poor people live, Paul declares in his mind. No one's hands built this furniture. The sisters won't pass the furniture on to the next generation. In two hundred years the bedroom furniture will still be worth less than a week's pay.

Theresa and Lisa have stuck little photos and ticket stubs in the crack between the mirror and the frame. The mementos remind him of amendments scribbled in the margins of an official document — the lease to a mid-size car or an announcement to change the zonage of a four-storey building. Paul has never seen one of these documents, but there must be millions of them in drawers all over Toronto.

It all depresses him. The city depresses him. He wishes he could leave. He's always wanted to move to England. He has to talk to Theresa about something or she'll fall asleep. She might wake up in a different mood. She might even sleep through the night.

"I had that dream again," he says.

They often have the same dreams: parties that end with a gory murder in a spare bedroom and only five minutes to bury the body before the police arrive; institutions with authority figures revealed as vampires, the sun about to set and legs that don't work; sitcoms of comic misunderstanding — "I thought this was *my* bed!" — that turn into snuff films.

In this dream, which he's been having since the spring, he is in a bathroom getting ready to go to a party. In the dream he admires himself in the mirror. He looks good, he knows it. His nose could be smaller, his eyes bluer, but that's okay, you have to work with what you got. He hates people who think they are prettier than they are.

I hate people who think than they are prettier they are. In the dream he imitates that pompous voice — his pompous voice — while he admires himself in the mirror. He realizes, with the certainty of any dream revelation, that all of his friends at the party are laughing at him. They are laughing at him, taking turns imitating his pompous voice. The shower curtain, superimposed from an apartment his family lived in just before he hit puberty, shows a pattern of plump naked women trying hard to look sensual and relaxed, as if being naked were the most natural thing in the world. They are cavorting in grapevines as thick as the women's arms. The grapes are big enough to be avocados. Paul is embarrassed and afraid for the women. He knows the terrible things that men say about women's bodies. He wants to open the curtain so he won't have to look at the women anymore. His face in the mirror is shadowed now. The party will be over by the time he gets there. A girl at the party who would have fallen in love with him will now leave with someone else. One of his lower front teeth has gone a little grey. The grey tooth looks like a tiny grease smudge on the mirror. He pulls down his bottom lip and touches the tooth. It is loose, irresistible. He pulls the tooth out. The other teeth tip toward the absence, holding their tilted position like a line of italicized prose, then they collapse and tumble, hanging from his gums on blue threads. He starts to pull all of his teeth out because if he pulls them out it will be easier to get dentures made. The dental plates will fit his gums better if all the teeth are missing. He is explaining this to someone.

Theresa laughs. "Could the symbolism be a little more obvious, please!"

She's right. The dream carries a bully of a message, a squat muscular symbol with no visible tipping point, no complexity to flatter, and a great hamhock of a hand protectively cupping its balls. "You're falling apart little man," the dream says.

"I need a new dream director," Paul says.

Theresa gives him a condescending smile. She's telling him to be tougher. She even kisses him on the cheek. But that's it, she's drifting off now, he can tell by her little satisfied smile. He might as well get ready to sleep. If they go to sleep this early they'll probably wake up by midnight and still have time to get the subway downtown for last call. They can phone Aida, see where that ends up.

Paul gets up for a long pee and looks at himself in the bathroom mirror until he is able to hold a neutral expression. He stands in the bedroom doorway. Theresa must be feeling a long sleep coming on because she has lit a last cigarette. The sun is shining almost straight through the bedroom window, congealing the smoke and humidity into a milky grey stratum between the bed and the ceiling. A second room is suspended in the air, opening into the air outside the window, four stories above the Allen Expressway. He imagines climbing into the floating room and walking right out the open window into a faerie land hanging above the city. Paul crawls back to the bed on his knees, obeying the borders of the floating room, and lies down on the bed. He lifts his hand to touch the floating room's outer wall without penetrating it. If he puts his hand in that room someone will grab it and pull him in and he will dance with the faeries in a circle for what feels like one night but will actually take thirty years off his life. In the morning Theresa will find him half-dead on the mattress, middle-aged and wild-eyed, babbling about the faerie dance. His mom read him a story about that. The book had a picture of a dandy with a long white beard and deep wrinkles, waking up in a forest clearing on a cold morning, the faeries long gone and laughing at his mortality.

Paul wishes he was high. He grabs the cigarette from Theresa and she smirks because, as they say at parties, *Paul doesn't smoke*. He takes an amateur's deep drag and blows paisleys of light and shade into the faerie room. He feels his follicles assert their hair in a long wave down his thighs. The floating room reminds him of something he knows he's never seen, something fine. Maybe books and movies and music have trained him to think that the room *should* remind him of something fine — of less conflicted times, maybe, of when he was a boy and pure of intention. But he's not conflicted. He was born to be in bed with Theresa, this woman who makes confident smoking noises with her mouth and breath. He looks for shadowy faces in the smoky air — a disapproving grandparent, or Richard — but the room is empty. Paul summons his deepest feelings — his love of a good laugh and the way his heart aches when he sees a lonely stranger on the bus — and sends those feelings into the floating room where they will be safe from his bad side. He wants his good feelings to go away from him for a while, to take a long rest and grow strong. Later, after he has been all over the world and suffered for his sins, he will go and live in the place his good feelings have prepared for him.

Theresa falls asleep and then Paul does. When they wake up it's dark. The floating room is gone.

It's cool enough to touch, so Paul spoons into Theresa. She pulls his hand under her ribs, wedging the lovers into a loose hug. He breathes onto the back of her neck because she loves that. Sometimes you do things just to make someone happy, he tells himself.

"Okay, what do you want from me?" she asks.

"Am I really that bad?"

"You wish."

And then there was the confetti on the floor. Hearing it finally mentioned, Jerome surrendered his head into his cupped hands. "I'll get to that later," he said. In another age his parents might have apprenticed him to a troupe of professional clowns to learn the full range of human folly; the best he could offer his friends was the full of his hungover face and a chance to play the role of sympathetic chorus by insisting that he didn't deserve to have these crazy things happen to him — at least not to the degree to which they'd been happening. "I mean — you guys know me."

"Oh, we know you," Matt said. "Too fucking well!"

The others laughed, remembering some anecdote that confirmed what they knew about Jerome. John reminded them of that night at Sneaky Dee's with the waitress. Ernie said, "The chick at the Pixies concert," and they laughed again.

"Come on," Jerome said. "I've done some of that stuff. But it's like Julie takes one thing in me, one *tendency*, and she makes that, like, my *leading feature*, like it's the thing that *rules* me. So I can't say to her, I never do that — because I'd be lying. But it's not like *she* says, either, because it's not as *bad* as she says, but it's not like she's lying either — because it's there, *in* me."

"And what *is* your first language, Jerome?" Matt asked.

"Are you translating directly from the fucking Hebrew?"

"He doesn't speak Hebrew."

"They kicked him out of the *shul* in grade six," Craig boasted.

"I speak Hebrew."

It was hot in Jerome's attic room. The windows were open, but an old maple tree on the front lawn kept the breeze out of the room and Jerome had packed his six electric fans into a box. They all remembered how Jerome used to arrange the fans around the room, one fan drawing air in through a window, a fan in each corner of the room to circulate the air, and one to push the old air out another window. Jerome explained to them once how he spent hours experimenting with the position of the fans to maximize the air flow, testing for drafts by lying on the bed with his shirt off — he insisted that breezes passing over exposed flesh caused colds, pinched nerves, and stiff muscles.

Jerome was always looking for an angle to improve his health. He refused to drink the city's tap water because of its supposed high chlorine ratio, and kept a case of bottled water under his bed and drank at least four bottles a day to "clean out his system." He reached under the bed and dragged the case out, then compressed his fingers into a funnel, stuck his hand through a narrow hole in the plastic casing, and pulled a bottle out by its neck, making the ripped plastic puff out like an exit wound.

Craig said the wounded plastic looked cool.

"I could just make the hole bigger."

"Pass the water that costs money," Matt said.

"You know, I pay so much money for this fucking stuff you'd think it would be old or something."

As they passed the bottle of water, the five friends thought about all the partying they'd done together, and it was as if they'd once fought side by side in a war, taking turns playing the part of the wounded private who urged the others to go on without him and the part of the corporal who carried his fallen brother to safety. They were veterans at twenty-two, though they had never worked together at a job that any of them cared about, or played on the same amateur sports team, or gone into business together. None had been the other's best man because none of them were married, and none had fathered a child to complain or brag about. They had never pooled skills passed down from fathers to fix up a car or a piece of property, and no one close to them had died or moved to another city, leaving the others to bond over an absence. But they had all met in their final days of sobriety and virginity, and they had taken turns driving each other's lingering enthusiasms out from the sheltering closets of private bedrooms, where these last ties to childhood were stomped to death with comedy routines extending over an entire summer. There was Craig's impersonation of Jerome at his telescope: "Look, I've discovered a new constellation — *Meps!* — shaped just like my sister's vaginer!" Jerome went after John's heavy-metal record collection with a shrieking falsetto: "Hello, North York! Do you want to rock and roll all night!?" The five friends remembered that summer as one long game of Gophers, where the carny gives you a pillowed stick and you have to clobber the stuffed gophers that pop their heads out of their holes for a split second, only here the stick had spikes on the end and the gophers were like children, slow and trusting, and when you smashed them they stayed dead.

The friends passed the bottle, and when the bottle came to John he drank from it without touching his lips to the rim. He did this by tilting his head back and holding the bottle a few inches above his open mouth. The manoeuvre was the first stage of a party trick John had invented years ago, which consisted of pouring wine or a slug of mixed drink into his mouth and then shooting the liquid into another party-goer's mouth through the gap in his front teeth. It really got things going at a party. John had played the trick on Claire the night they met. He'd seen her standing alone at a party scanning the alphabetized spines in a big bookcase. The bookcase was made out of good wood, with the shelves built into the frame. The soft couch had been covered with a tasteful quilt for the party, and there were side tables that hadn't been found in the garbage or snagged at a lawn sale. John realized that he was starting to go to parties with people who carefully selected their furniture and bookcases, and that made him a little proud of himself and sentimental. He also felt guilty remembering that he had deliberately not invited any of his friends to come with him. He took his rye and ginger and walked over to the woman looking at the book spines and made a joke about some of the translated German novels on the middle shelf. She surprised him by cracking an even funnier joke.

John was suddenly half-sober. "I came over here to do a party trick on you," he said.

"What's the trick?"

"It only works if I can trick you into opening your mouth first."

"Go ahead."

"How many fillings do you have?"

"Seven," she said.

"I don't believe you. Let me see."

He got her. They spent the rest of the party leaning together against the bookcase making fun of people, her daring him to shoot booze into people's mouths, he daring her to steal an old copy of Knut Hamsen's *Pan*, which she did. He hadn't shot booze into anyone's mouth since.

John saw now that his friends were watching him pour the water into his mouth. They didn't want him to shoot water into their mouths through the gap in his teeth, but they watched him closely, as if they were expecting him to demonstrate a new party trick. John guessed what they were thinking, so he tipped his head back and poured the last of the bottle into his mouth and made a loud gargling noise that he punctuated with a belch. No one laughed. He'd let his friends down. "It's like this," he wanted to say, but he wouldn't know how to finish the sentence. He knew what they were thinking — that Claire had domesticated him or he had domesticated her and now he hardly went out at night with his friends. Explaining that working five nights a week in a bar had put him off partying wouldn't have done any good — John didn't believe the argument himself.

Jerome looked like shit. He was hungover, tired from the unexpected sex, and probably wondering the price he would pay for the sudden reinsertion of Julie into his life. His friends were waiting for him to list these high-water marks of pandemonium and then toss an imaginary sheaf of papers into the air and say, "Let's do this fucking move and then let's get drunk." Jerome took out another bottle of water and opened it. He seemed to be waiting for his friends to force him, through another round of insults, to pack the rest of his stuff and bring the van to the front of the house.

After the second bottle of water did the rounds Craig pointed to the confetti on the floor. "You been fucking a clown, Jerome?"

"When he cums a cannon fires confetti all over the room."

"All right." Jerome raised his hands into a "halt" position.

"Hey, I thought you vowed not to sleep with Julie again," John said.

Jerome looked relieved that John had brought this up. "I

did. But we went out last night."

"Ergo the confetti!"

"Ergo hardly any fucking boxes packed. She left just before you guys got here. We were fucking about two hours ago."

"Give me a quarter so I can call my editor at the city desk!"

Jerome laughed with them this time, slipping in an "Oh, it's true," between his big, sink-backing-up laughs. "Man, we came back from Ecuador in June and we more or less broke up, and she did her thing and I did mine, and *fuck*, we just ended up seeing each other last night. How long it'll last I don't know. But it means a lot of good sex. You know —" he made a chopping motion "— it's like when I see her I automatically get pulled in again. Insert sex joke here."

"Now, Jerome," Ernie said, stretching the "o" so that Jerome's name drooped in the middle like a wiener dog. "Even you must be noticing a pattern here. Jerome, are you one of those guys who's in love with love?" The others were already laughing, deepening Ernie's commitment to a straight face. "I think you're one of those highly emotional men — too much time with your mother maybe. You love the anticipation of a new relationship — *does she really love ME?* The romance of thinking that she's The One, the whole drama of dumping her when you realize she isn't even The Two, and then the make-up sex, all the while carrying on the same relationship with three other women."

Craig clapped. "Holy shit!"

"Check your underwear: you've been unmanned," Matt said.

Jerome loved hearing his life dramatized into anecdotes, even when they made him look like an idiot, but it looked like Ernie had gone too far. Jerome dropped his head back into his hands and then surprised them by waving his right hand in a come-forward motion, as if Ernie were a truck backing into a loading bay to unload a dreaded but necessary cargo.

"Jerome, you don't need a pop psychologist to tell you this. You can't base your love life on fights and make-up sex."

"That's the fun part," Craig said.

"Who told you relationships were supposed to be fun?"

"The first few dates are fun."

"*Dates*." Matt said. "You've never taken a girl on a date in your life." Matt never tired of presenting evidence of Craig's unearned successes with women to a packed imaginary court-room.

"Okay. The first few times they take me home are fun."

"The first dates are fun because there's no relationship yet," Ernie said. "It's like when you start a new job at a factory. It's kind of interesting for the first half-hour, then it becomes a hideous display of boredom until you're walking around all day and night with that factory strapped to your back like an eighteen-ton weight."

They laughed at that. John was laughing at Ernie, who'd been going out with the same woman longer than any of them — more than three years. Ernie didn't want his friends thinking that anything in life made him happy. He ran down his relationship with Linda without ever specifying what it was he didn't like about it. He doted on Linda by criticizing her in a way that didn't make her look bad in front of the guys. She bought most of Ernie's shirts for him, and played relationship counsellor to his friends, and kept his drinking under control, except on the nights when she bought a bottle of gin and announced that, tonight, it was her turn to get wasted. Ernie would roll his eyes and say, "Lock up your sons and grandsons," or "Make sure you wear your bib, dar-ling," all the while radiating anticipation at the thought of a drunk Linda ranting and mocking the boys, dancing and playing the stereo too loud, bugging John to shoot gin into her mouth through the gap in his teeth.

Over time and drinks John must have told his friends enough about Claire so that if she were murdered a detective questioning them would get an accurate picture of John and Claire's love life, minus the crucial fact that could finger John for the murder: he hadn't been able to make Claire cum for the first year they were sleeping together. She enjoyed sex — probably more than he did. Sex for him was a hysterical argument between his eyes, cock, and heart as they lurched across the table of Claire's body trying to grab the biggest portion. Sex was a holding back, a brisk walk across a slippery floor carrying a tray of full pitchers he was forbidden to spill. Beneath him Claire was as graceful as a water mammal. There she was at night, moving beneath him — eyes closed over a private smile, murmuring his name and whispering to herself, as if she were in a disciplined half sleep that never collapsed into unconsciousness. She went to a place without corners or edges or time, and it made him envious. They would be fucking and she would suddenly nudge him onto his back and ride him. He was her trapeze bar, her tightrope and adoring audience as she rode him to a place beyond orgasms. Elevated above him, she was a kind of angel, a spirit of light and sound, while he lay flesh-heavy on the bed. John would dig foot caves in the blankets and try to push himself deeper into her, pinching himself hard on the back of his leg to stop himself from cumming. She pulled him closer when he was about to cum, their arms and legs complementary puzzle pieces. For a half-second he seemed to fuse with her, but when he came she was pulled from his arms, as if he'd abandoned her on some rocky crag to guard the oxygen tank while he climbed the last fifty feet of the mountain to view the great distances of the world.

John told her about this. He said it wasn't fair for her.

Claire told him not to worry, that orgasms didn't really matter to her. "Sex is like a story that just goes on and on for me," she told him. John didn't believe her, he saw himself as the lightweight husband comforted by his buxom wife in the old Playboy cartoons he'd studied as a child. His orgasms, his easy surrender to bright lights and groans, summed up their entire relationship, how he always needed to find the beginning and ending of things and his cue to join in, and how she was just a part of things as they happened, some vital limb of the body of every event that passed through their shared life.

This envy of Claire made John more self-conscious in bed, which helped him hold off his own orgasm longer, which made her enjoy sex even more. Claire seemed to climb even higher above him, until one night she began making whimpering noises that made him worry he was hurting her. She held onto his shoulders as if she were afraid she was going to be lifted away from him. She looked into his eyes, pleading for him to not stop what he was doing to her. He'd never seen her look so vulnerable. It made him want to cry. He held her tighter. She kept saying, "*OH*," as if something important and very obvious were being explained to her. Then Claire looked down at him again — the beautiful Claire that he loved — wearing the surprised and happy face of the lonely child walking into a surprise party thrown in her honour. Then she said, "*Yes*," and a dozen other affirmations as a wave moved through her over and over again. She kept kissing every inch of him that her lips could reach.

When he finally came, his orgasm felt a prolonged but pleasant hiccup. This had happened almost two weeks earlier. John had made Claire cum three more times since. Now he kept asking himself why he couldn't cum like she did.

There was no way he could talk to his friends about this. No fucking way. And he wondered if it was like this for all men.

Jerome kept looking around the room and reaching the same conclusion: the move was too tedious to even contemplate. He pulled the clock-radio plug out of the wall and said, "When I want your opinion I'll fucking ask for it."

In spite of what Jerome had said earlier, almost all of his possessions were packed into boxes — his books, computer equipment, most of his knick-knacks. The three large plants he'd cultivated since he was a teenager were lined up under the north window, as far away from the boxes as the room allowed, probably to remind himself to save the plants for the last load. His posters had been rolled and his framed The Kids Are All Right movie poster draped in a blanket. Jerome couldn't do a job without doing it well. He had packed the boxes neatly, with breakables wrapped in stray items of clothing and placed between heavy items unlikely to bounce around during the move. Only the area around his bed needed organizing, and some of his food was still shelved in the communal kitchen.

Jerome was probably putting off the trip to the kitchen. He had fallen out with one of his female housemates. He had tried to explain what happened to John, calling it an extended case of crossed intentions, of misread hints and games that turned serious. "It was like some fucking sitcom," he told John, "where Mr. Roper overhears Jack and Chrissy talking about a cake they're going to bake that night, but Mr. Roper only hears half of what they've said — you know, how Jack and Chrissy can't wait to *lick the icing off the whipping stick*, and Mr. Roper thinks *lick the whipping stick* is slang for a blow job and that the two of them are planning an orgy. Then when they invite Mr. Roper over for dessert he freaks out. You know how it is." He liked playing with people, he said, but you can't flirt with these feminist chicks.

Claire was an exception, he said, she didn't hate being a woman.

The phone rang. Jerome gripped his legs, as if afraid they were going to flee the sound of the ringer. His eyes were bloodshot. He picked up the phone and listened before saying hello. There was no one on the other end. "That's been happening a lot lately."

His friends resisted the easy punchlines.

"Oh, more of the latest news for you guys: that phone call was probably from the ghost of Helena." He looked at John. "You remember I told you about her?"

John nodded. Helena's details: manic depressive, talented artist, exotic-looking — Jerome couldn't help himself.

Jerome made a slicing motion across his neck. "She really did it this time."

"Offed herself?

"Hung herself from a tree in High Park. That happened during this weird spell of events that ended with me fucking Julie."

Craig asked.

"Helena was this artist from Poland I knew, a real manic type. Her art was fucking amazing."

"And you fucked her," Matt said.

"A couple of times last summer, yeah. Nothing serious. Helena tried to kill herself a couple of times — really tried, even jumped off a bridge once."

"Shit."

"Fate always crept in and, *uh*, they kept saving her. Not this time. Now I keep getting these phone calls where no one is on the other end. I think it's her." He nodded. "You know what I mean," he said. Jerome was not asking them to believe that her ghost was on the other end of the line — though he couldn't say that it wasn't — but that her death and her art and her character and its entanglement in his life had triggered enough strange correspondences to somehow make his phone ring.

"If you have enough appliances or computers and stuff turned on at the same time, you get static electricity and all kinds of *spillage*," Jerome said. "Remember that storm two weeks ago? Just before the lightning came, I had my fans going and my computer and stereo on, and I swear that little electric car that I bought for my nephew's birthday actually started by itself. I nearly shit myself."

"She hung herself from a tree? Wow." Craig nodded decisively, as though confirming some long-running theory about integrity.

"I'd never been to a funeral before," Jerome said. His voice had become matter of fact, a sign that he was about to describe an unsettling experience. "Never seen a dead person, actually. When I went to the viewing — it was open coffin — I'd always heard about this *thing*, and I wondered if it was true, that in the case of violence they do things to cover up any visible marks. If it's a suicide for instance."

They all wanted to know.

"They had this beautiful handkerchief around her neck."

They all nodded at the floor or found some other way to leave Jerome to his thoughts.

John was pretty sure he'd never met Helena. He remembered Jerome telling him about this artist chick he'd just slept with. Jerome had assured him that everything was cool, that Helena was too into her art to care about what he got up to with other women. John knew what he had wanted to say to Jerome: "You know how this is all going to end? She'll feel betrayed and you'll say it wasn't your fault — you never *promised* her anything." John had wanted to tell Jerome that he must be noticing a pattern here, that every woman who told him that she didn't care about what he got up to with other women ended up hating him when she found out what he got up to with other women. He wanted to tell Jerome that maybe his lovers didn't mean what they were saying, that they were like kids who tell their friends that they're not afraid of ghosts before climbing the wall of the local graveyard. Of course the kids are afraid of ghosts, what would be the point of breaking into the graveyard if they weren't afraid, and of course your lover minded what you did with other women, why else would she want to be your lover?

If John had been Ernie he would have told Jerome straight out that he was the cause of his own problems and that he had to either stick to one-night stands or one-woman relationships, never mind this have-your-cake-and- eat-it-too shit. But if John *was* Ernie, Jerome wouldn't have confided in him about Helena in the first place; he would have found a friend as easygoing as John and told *him* about Helena. That was the price of being nice: you could never stop being nice. On the rare occasions that John was completely honest with people, he always ended up saying too much. He sounded like he was delivering a final judgment on the other person's life — at least that's how people took what he was saying.

The room was still silent, as if they had agreed to observe a period of silence in honour of Helena without setting a time limit for that silence. John lifted his head just enough to bring Jerome into view, hoping to catch him in one of those rare moments when his attention wasn't being manhandled by the outside world. Jerome was looking out the window over Craig's head. Jerome's face was incapable of a neutral expression — his eyebrows were chiselled above his eyes, his forehead swelled like the base of a dome. His face looked constipated now, stuck, as if an expression had gotten trapped in the netting of his facial muscles. Jerome looked around the room and said, "I guess the Helena story dropped a downer on all our talk about fucking," scoring the biggest laugh of the afternoon.

"Speaking of which," Craig said, "I fucked Stacy again." He waited for a response, the congratulatory ribbing they'd given Jerome over Julie.

Matt smirked. "*Stacy*. Racy, spacy Stacy!"

"She broke into my house with a case of beer the other night," Craig said, as if this act would redeem her, once and for all time, in his friends' eyes. "She climbed onto the little roof over the kitchen and through my window. She makes the beer herself."

"Brewmaster Stacy," Matt said.

"And what does her boyfriend think about that?" Ernie said.

"She goes home to him and he looks after her. He's her daddy. I'm just her thing on the side, her boy."

"How European."

No one believed that Craig was happy being Stacy's boy. He had gotten very attached to her 3 a.m. phone calls and guerilla sex, her scenes in crowded bars that her beauty almost let her get away with. He loved having a lover that other women hated, a lover cut off from her own gender. His friends wouldn't bug him so much about her if he would just admit that he got off on the whole thing.

"She hasn't started buying into your doomed poet shtick?" Matt said.

"She's too smart for that — that's what I like about her."

"Smart or not, it doesn't mean she's not stupid."

"You just have to get to know her better."

"Craig likes to get to know a girl, all right," Ernie said. "His specialty is slowly peeling away their thin veneer of rationality to reveal the blithering idiot underneath."

"Unlike Craig himself," Matt said, "who is always willing to show the world his blithering idiot underneath in all its glory!"

"Hey, the women fall for it."

"They can relate."

"I'm an idiot all the time and I don't have any trouble getting laid. It makes you wonder if clowns have groupies." The joke didn't throw them off his trail. "I haven't actually acted like an idiot with Stacy. I'm very cool with her."

"But that's exactly how you act like an idiot: by being cool," John said.

"No, man, this is a masterpiece. I'm a god in her eyes."

"In *whose* eyes?"

"Never in my eyes. That's why I have to content myself being a god in their eyes."

"Are you a god in my eyes, Craig?" Matt asked.

"I don't care how I look in your eyes, Matt — God knows I don't want to want fuck *you*. Now, John, on the other hand. . . ."

They all laughed when Craig grabbed John's thigh, relieved that Craig wasn't going to make any more cracks about Matt's latest bout of involuntary celibacy, a topic they had consigned to some shuttered pen beyond the reach of their jokes. It was cheap for Craig to even bring it up, but Matt had it coming for riding him so hard about Stacy.

John leaned forward in his chair and lifted his shirt to air his chest and back. He wanted something to eat, but offering to order a pizza might snap Jerome out of his hangover, reminding him that they should have started packing his stuff into the van over an hour ago. John didn't want to be the one to call them all to work — they'd all think that he was being a drag, trying to hurry things along so he could go back home and see Claire.

He had been telling Claire that morning that he resented having to spend his day off helping Jerome move his stuff —

the third time in less than two years, in case anyone was counting. He said he never should have told the guys how much he enjoyed working as a mover that summer after high school. He was lying in bed with her drinking tea. "Now every time one of them moves they just figure I'll help," he said. She reminded him that he could just say no. "No," he said, "you always have to help your friends when they ask." The consequence of not helping a friend seemed to take form as an invisible presence pressing down on him from above the bed. He was reminded by the room's lack of decoration that he and Claire rented this apartment from a man who owned a string of rundown houses, and somehow the man became connected with the bad things that could happen to a person who didn't stick by their friends. John said to Claire — as if he'd just passed up the opportunity to do so — that even if he owned his own business he wouldn't hire one of his friends. "I wouldn't want to be put in that position. I'd just give him whatever money he needed," he assured her.

She must have meant something different because she said, "The only reason they're all still friends is because of you. They have to have you there."

He reminded her that the guys did lots of stuff without him — Craig and Matt went for cheap fajitas every Tuesday, Jerome and Ernie jammed.

She said he was funny and told him not to be stupid, he knew what she meant.

John knew he was going to end up getting drunk with them tonight — he'd never hear the end of it if he didn't. He touched the left pocket of his cut-offs, which held a wad of small bills encased in its green sausage skin of twenties. It was one night's worth of tips, and he'd just worked five nights in a row. He had a wad of bills as thick as a hero sandwich in the night table by his side of the bed. Every second

Friday he deposited his tips into a shared bank account that Claire looked after, and though he had agreed to this arrangement he couldn't shake the feeling that depositing the money into the account was slowing down their rate of financial accumulation. He would take out the bank book and look at the numbers in the balance column, the creeping digits slowly turning over in their sleep, and he'd swear that they should more money than that in the bank. It was as if the bank book, with its lines and headings and sober cover, was diminishing the value of their money without actually subtracting from the balance.

Some mornings after Claire went to work he would open the drawer next to his side of the bed and press the pile of bills into a tight gunpowder cap, the height of which he measured with his pointing finger: two digits of untaxed income from two weeks of tips. At this rate he could have a stack of bills as high as his waist in a year. He knew it was stupid, but he couldn't and didn't want to shake the feeling that a pile of bills as high as his waist would be worth more than however many digits he and Claire could run up in the balance column of their bank account. He liked thinking about money that way, that the bills and coins were like grain that you could store for the winter.

A couple of days earlier, after Claire left for work, John had taken the two-week wad of tips and thrown the money on the bed to see what shape the pile would make. He expected to see money flowers, a Rorschach blot, paper entrails snaking into the future, but the bills just looked spilled, as if they'd been poured out of a broken jar and now lay on the bed in the second stage of a theft. He spread the bills out and then arranged them in rows until he had what looked like a multicoloured quilt covering most of the bed. He thought to himself, This is how the rich sleep at night, under blankets of money. It was a child's fantasy of plenty.

John didn't care. The money quilt reminded him of the child he'd been — the allowance hoarder, the boy whose first pornography was the jewellery section of the Eaton's Christmas catalogue. Remembering the catalogue invited the child he had been into the room. The boy did not hold John's hand, but he stood close enough to close the air between them. John and the boy smiled down at the quilt, playing a game to see who could hold their eyes open the longest without blinking. John was winning. The quilt's colours were shifting like the skin of a good log burning in a fireplace. John blinked and said to the boy, "Look at all this fucking money! We can buy anything we want. What do you want to buy?" John had just taken a shower. He was naked under his robe and he and Claire had fooled around to no conclusion the night before — "light petting" she called it, comfort food.

John took off his robe, his erection shooing the boy from the room. He was only going to lie on the money and throw a few handfuls of bills into the air, a bankrobber with his loot in a motel on the free side of the State line. He could see himself telling the guys about it: "I had a money bath — one more childhood fantasy to check off the list." (His erection would not make an appearance in the story.) But as he lay down on his stomach, his heavy shoulders and thighs settling into money, and the smell of Claire beneath the money, and the bills' government smoothness like a wallet around his cock took hold of him. He rolled on his side and began to jerk off. He didn't conjure any dirty pictures. He didn't cry out for a girl he couldn't have. He didn't think about Claire. He was fucking the feeling of being a boy again, the illusion that he had enough money to buy a castle and take a trip around the world and buy the whole Eaton's catalogue. It only took a minute. When he came his legs pantomimed a man running across a flowered field to greet a long-lost love, sending a few bills into the air, the paper money shot quietly floating down and settling over his bare calves. He had ejaculated onto a pair of twenties, which he barely wiped off and spent later that day at a used-clothing store in the Market, pressing the glazed bills into the hand of the rock-star wannabe behind the cracked glass display case of silver jewellery.

He touched the money through his pants again. He took the bills out and waved the roll under his own nose. "One night's bounty."

"How much?" Matt asked.

"I don't know." John wasn't bragging — he hadn't expected anyone to ask. He fanned out the money and held it up to his friends.

Craig grabbed the money. "Here, I'll spend it for you," he said and rubbed the money against his crotch. "Suck it, bitch!"

Everyone but John laughed. Matt and Craig laughed longer than they needed to, chewing over and passing from mouth to mouth some in-joke not bound for the communal pot. John saw them pass the look. They were marking a space in a private conversation they would have when they were alone. John grabbed the money from Craig's hand, pinched his nipple hard, and stuffed a five-dollar bill into Craig's T-shirt.

"Buy yourself something pretty," John said, knowing that Craig would take the money because he was so broke. He would take the money and still mock John later. John wasn't trying to buy Craig's respect or anything, but the guy could at least show some fucking gratitude.

Craig said, "Did I ever tell you guys about my friends, Mike and Tony?"

He hadn't.

Craig wiped his thick lips and pulled at his long curly hair and sniffed a few times. He was like a dog flattening the grass before he settled down to a long nap. His friends let him get away with the drama because they loved hearing his stories. Craig nodded a few times, pretending to recall a few more details of the story, then he spoke. "Mike and Tony were the Muillet brothers. They were aces at stealing porno mags from the Woolco, which is some other chain store now. I'd go in there with them and buy a Coke or whatever, and while I was doing that at the counter Mike and Tony would stuff a few porn mags down their pants — each. We had the greatest porno stash in the ravine."

"That's the fort in the ravine you were talking about before?" John asked.

"Yeah, but we were smart, we didn't keep them in the fort. We wrapped them in grocery bags and buried them near the fort. Problem was Tony kept forgetting where we'd buried them. We lost so many magazines that way but then we'd just steal other guys' porno stashes. It was great, we'd just go through the woods looking for fresh piles of dirt and dig down — bingo, a bag of porn, just like a fucking faerie tale. And it was usually disgusting stuff, none of this girl-next-door being sexy for her special man. I'm talking Tits 'n Snatch and Split Beaver Monthly."

Craig's friends remembered being alone behind closed doors, turning the pages of a porn mag, wanting to see what else the naked women could do, relieved that the women kept doing the same thing. They remembered the sensation of their bodies being entered, through the eyes, by a kind of demon that set their minds on fire with possibilities. The curve of one woman's breast, the nipple of another, the light resting in the hollow of a full hip: these were the footholds of a ladder to a new world of action and mystery. The demon showed them these footholds, but their bodies were not ready step onto the ladder. The boys pulled and prodded and rubbed their cocks, trying to make something happen, trying to take that first step onto the ladder into that other world. But they couldn't reach the ladder, so they ran out onto their lawns to start fights with their friends and deal out noogies and taunt the weak. They mounted their bikes and raced down steep ravine trails half-hoping for a glorious death impaled on a tree branch. They lay in bed at night thinking about the women, thinking about war and death on the battlefield.

Craig gave them time to remember those days, the dirty magazines. He must have been thinking about all this for awhile. "The most grotesque possible way to learn about sex, eh? I remember in grade eight my old man finally decided to have the *sex talk* with me."

His friends were already laughing.

"There I am with three years of hardcore sex viewing under my belt and he starts telling me about making babies, and I'm like, Dad, I know all that stuff, don't worry. The only question I asked him was, 'Dad, what's an enema?'"

They joined in: "Dad, why would a woman want to suck off a donkey?"

"Dad, why do hot bitches want to fuck all night?"

"Yeah," Craig said, "here's my dad talking about babies and I already know — vicariously — how to finger a girl's clit. There were these two guys in my neighbourhood, both named Sylvain, who lived next door to each other. Sylvain, the older one, claimed to be getting fucked all the time. He explained the mysteries of the clit to us. He said something like, 'Don't crush the worm.'"

They groaned.

"Yeah, fuck, eh? Once we knocked on Sylvain's front door and he wasn't home so, I don't know why, we decided to look into his basement window. There he was," Craig made a jerking-off motion and crossed his eyes. "Yessir, he was chokin' it. So we started cheering him on and he saw us and freaked out and Sylvain came out and beat the shit out of Sylvain."

John was still thinking about the magazines. He said, "Do you think that fucked you up for sex?"

"Seeing a guy jerk off? I watch you guys doing it every time you open your mouths."

"No, the porn and the . . ." John couldn't think of the word. He was watching a memory of himself humping the carpet through his jeans on the floor of his brother's bedroom. John had found his brother's porno stash, and though he studied every dirty picture, he always returned to the same three women — blonde, voluptuous, bored with their own beauty and the jewellery-bestowing men who desired it.

"The porn," he said, "all those pictures of women getting off, acting it out — women just existing in this world of sex and loving it." He thought of Claire, and he saw Claire's beautiful body and wondered if he would still love her if she wasn't beautiful. He didn't just love her because she was beautiful — he had dated good-looking women and loved them a lot less than he loved her. But Claire's beauty was the trigger of his love, the trigger and the gunpowder. He couldn't think about her without thinking about her body and her face and her smell and the way she moved. What did that say about him?

"Sure it fucked me up," Craig said. He was tentative. Ernie and Matt and Jerome weren't interested in the conversation. They shifted in their seats, making stretching gestures with their upper backs and shoulders.

"It fucked *me* up, I think," John said. He didn't care if they didn't want to talk about this. He knew they were all thinking about the porn they'd worshipped when they were boys. "You look at the porn," he said, "and you're given all this information, laid out on the page, like an anatomy book about sex, and you still don't learn anything about women. Seriously, have you ever thought about how it must feel for women?" John stopped himself, aware that he had been leading the conversation to this point. "Like, when they cum," he said. "Like, you know, I remember the first time Claire had an orgasm." By saying "I remember" John was placing the orgasm into a sequence of sexual events without tying it down to the calendar. He was telling his friends what had happened between Claire and him without having to tell them that she'd only cum for the first time a week ago. "I mean, I thought I'd killed her at first. She went crazy, I thought I'd hurt her, then I thought she'd never want to stop fucking."

Craig jumped in: "Yeah, Stacy calls me by these fucked-up names when she cums. Seriously, she grabs my head and says these cryptic phrases like, 'Do you know? Tell me Craig, do you *know*?' Then she cries."

Everyone was laughing. Ernie, instead of hinting that John and Craig's lovers exaggerated their orgasms for inscrutable feminine purposes that they would later use to their advantage, only nodded. "Man, their orgasms put us to shame," he said. "Sometimes when Linda cums I feel like I could get up, go make myself a sandwich, come back in the room, and she'd still be thrashing in the sheets calling my name. Man, I get so jealous."

Matt and Jerome nodded, uniting the room. John decided that he was going to get very drunk with his friends that night. A thousand party stories starring his friends crowded the lip of his consciousness. He was going to go out and get wasted with his friends and not care about where he ended up crashing for the night. He was more fun when he was drunk, funnier — he could make anyone laugh. When he was drunk he jumped on parked cars and dived into thorny hedges, laughing. He cried when he was drunk. He gave the last of his money to street people.

He said, "I'm buying the first two pitchers tonight."

Jerome said, "I'm buying the rest. Just don't ask me to feed you fuckers."

Jerome's roommate arrived with a pot of coffee and some styrofoam cups left over from a house party. Jerome said, "I guess we've earned a coffee break," and went downstairs to borrow some milk and a handful of sugar cubes. When he came back in the room he was carrying a box of spices and a litre of milk. He had passed through the worst stages of his hangover and would expect them to start working soon. He poured the coffee and began putting some knick-knacks into a half-filled box.

Everyone but Matt complimented the coffee, which the roommate had bought from the organic food co-op just down the street. Jerome said that he had made plans at least a dozen times to go and join the co-op but never got around to doing it, he didn't know why. You had to give the co-op a small deposit and pay an even smaller annual fee, and you had to work at the store a couple of hours a month, which might be fun and a cool way to meet people.

Matt said, "I thought you were sworn off those leftie chicks."

Jerome nodded and said, *still*, he did want to meet new people, a different type from the ones he'd been meeting the last couple of years. The way he said it implied that the kind of person he'd been meeting had contributed to his present sorry state. He tried to describe this new kind of person, saying they should be "interesting" and "in the world," before settling on the roommate who'd brought them the coffee as a typical, if not perfect, example.

"I mean, you look at him and think, *fuck* — peasant cap, granny glasses, beard — he's a fucking hippie," Jerome said. "And it's sort of true. But he's interesting. He plays the guitar, he's got some interesting albums and books, and him and these friends of his go to a farmhouse a lot of week- ends." As if to prove that his soon-to-be-former roommate also had a practical side Jerome explained how he went to Nepal twice a year and imported clothes into Canada.

"I mean, I don't want to look like the guy," Jerome assured them. "But I'm glad I got to know him, you know? I mean, I'll keep in contact."

"Our Jerome is growing up," Matt said.

Matt was being dismissive and cynical. Jerome wasn't having any of it. He packed the case of water into a box and said, "Yeah, well, I'm getting sick of this." He looked around the room and saw that his friends looked hurt. "Of moving," he said, just to clear things up.

A CONFUSION OF ISLANDS

Every evening I played a game as I walked down to Commercial Drive. Across the Burrard Inlet the houses on the north shore and up Grouse Mountain were coming on. I had two minutes to think up an analogy to describe the lights or I had to take a quarter out of my pocket and throw it down a sewer from a distance of three feet.

The first night I played the lights were votive candles on an altar. Later they became holes in the mountain letting out faerie light; then a blanket of stars; then a landing strip designed to confuse pilots. Tonight the air was hazy, and the lights became the torches of angry North Vancouverites climbing the mountain to finally murder the monster in Frankenstein's castle.

Ray, dragging a hockey bag and couple of suitcases — his worldly possessions pared down to a three-bag greatest-hits collection of books, clothes, and cassettes — was going to get off the Greyhound bus from Toronto the next day. He would quote a line from *On the Road*, a book we'd outgrown years before but that still clung to us by threads of irony, and I would tell him about my new but still larval life in Vancouver, about this new man I'd become, a sober man who read in cafés and wrote apologetic letters to ex-lovers. And Ray was going to laugh and laugh.

I was looking for an old hippie named Danny, one of the few native Vancouverites I'd met since arriving. The relationship was part of a resolution to widen my social world beyond the cliques of ex-patriot Torontonians who crowded the Italian coffee bars along Commercial Drive. All conversations there led back to the favoured scapegoat: Toronto, inevitably described as hollow, greedy, grasping — a "city of rats" was my favourite. When pressed to describe their new home city, the exiles resorted to a hazier spectrum of clichés. Vancouver was integrated, laid-back, holistic — character traits that formed a composite sketch of the sandal-wearing Everyman they hoped to become. This was my Vancouver, then, an updated, low-rent Edwardian sanitorium where the disillusioned intelligentsia came to take the cure and write fractured free verse. The hippies couldn't offer much worse.

I found Danny outside the food co-op, sitting at one of the wicker patio tables with a few younger hippies. Danny and a litter of puppies lived in a van parked near the community centre. His cheeks and nose were covered in an angry rash — his skin actually looked angry at the indignities it had suffered: nights sleeping out, days without soap or suntan lotion, the heat of exploding capillaries. Danny liked to play the part of elder statesman to folks passing through Vancouver on their way to the islands. But his ruined cheeks, the sour smell of van and dog clinging to his body, and his open lust for very young women rendered him a kind of anti-prophet, his life story — especially the pivotal rejection of a career in academia for a three-year acid binge on Vancouver Island — a cautionary tale. Which meant the suddenly tolerant younger hippies sitting with him at the table were here for the same reason as me: to volunteer to help drive Danny's van down to an annual "barter fair" in Washington state.

Like many drug casualties, Danny's ability to detect condescension had expanded in direct proportion to the withering of his other mental functions. If I chose the wrong tone or gesture, Ray and I would never get a spot in the van.

"I got arrested for impaired driving this morning," Danny told me.

"You said your licence was already suspended."

"I was just *sitting* in my goddamned van and the fucking cops busted me!"

Everybody else was drained of outrage, having probably heard the story at least six times. I feigned shock, gaining Danny's full attention.

"I thought they were going to try and take my puppies away, so I said, 'I'd rather have six puppies than a hundred pigs!' They fucking beat the shit out of me!" He made a violent lean in the direction of the girl on his left, giving her the full blast of his breath. "They beat me in forced confinement." The memory of a 1970s' feminist consciousness-raising session seemed to waft up in him. "I know what it's like to be raped. I know what it's like to be a woman!"

"Great," she said, "but are you going to be able to get across the border with that ID?"

Danny pulled back from the repelled bonding moment. He looked relieved, as if the girl's sarcasm had freed him from the memory of a time when he had tried to be a better man. "Don't worry about the ID, I got it made in my brother's name. His record's clean. He's a Jehovah's Witness, eh." He pulled out a generic ID card.

"Yeah, so my name's Dave. That's my brother's name." Danny turned to me. "Your buddy's gonna have to do a lot of driving."

Ray immediately assumed the role of long-suffering rationalist to Danny's stoner hippie in the sitcom episode that was our drive to the border. Ray was driving. Danny was in the passenger seat hoarding the map, already drunk on a bottle of homemade wine. I was sitting on a milk crate between them. Six of us had shown up at Danny's van at ten that morning, only to find him passed out and unwakeable for almost two hours. It took Danny another two hours to get ready, then we got lost three times driving out to the suburbs to drop off his puppies at his brother's house. When I asked to see the map Danny sneered and said, "This isn't Toronto."

Ray, even more hungover than I was, started repeating the last few words of Danny's sentences.

"Okay, now turn left at that variety store."

"At that variety store, yup."

"There should be a Laundromat up here, eh."

"Yeah, a Laundromat."

I had told Ray the night before that a weekend with a camp full of hippies was the perfect initiation to his new West Coast life. "Think of the weekend as an inoculation against further infection," I said. Ray looked surprised that I felt the need to convince him to go. He didn't care if the campsite was going to be full of hippies. The important thing was that we were going to America, his spiritual homeland, decadent land of guns and body fat and swagger and home to most of his favourite authors: Burroughs, John Fante, Bukowski. The trip would also help us put off looking for jobs for another few days.

We reached the border and took our place behind about a dozen cars. Danny began to eat a peanut-butter sandwich to take the smell of alcohol off his breath. "Ray," he said. "RAY. Remember, my name's Dave."

"Can you tell me three more times so I can dream about it tonight?"

"And the name of the guy who owns the van is Russell Copp. Like 'police-cop' with an extra 'p'."

"I thought it was your van."

"It is, but I never changed the papers. So just say that Russell Copp is the owner of the van. He went tree-planting and lent us his van."

"Everyone get ready for a cavity search!" I shouted.

"Listen to the Toronto fucking comedians, eh," Danny said to the back of the van where the four young hippies were sitting. "They must be trying out their new routine on us."

Ken, a quiet guy with dreads who kept writing in a journal, said that maybe we should let Darlene drive over the border. Darlene was a nineteen-year-old tree planter with the kind of cherubic features that authority figures want to protect and/or molest. I was already developing a crush on her, reconfiguring all of my potential futures to include an invigorating love affair with a young free spirit. I would grow to love Darlene's easy laugh as we travelled across America, me guarding her too-open heart while the hard ball of cynicism in my guts softened like a beeswax candle in the afternoon sun of her love. We would settle in for the winter on a rustic farm near the Pacific Ocean, where I would I write my first novel, which I would dedicate to her healing love. I reminded myself that this was exactly the type of easy fantasizing that I had moved out to Vancouver to cure myself of.

With Darlene at the helm, the guard waved us through without asking who owned the van.

There were yellow ribbons tied on the trees in America, though the Gulf War had ended months earlier. The ribbons were still bright and untattered, like a saint's relics, impervious to rot, or roses that grow in winter in a faerie tale. Flags as big as Buicks hung from poles carefully set at the same noble tilt as the raising of Old Glory at Iwo Jima.

Out on the interstate, the road cut through the trees like a railway through a wilderness frontier, with only the odd turnoff sign to remind drivers of the American towns huddling behind the trees. At predictable intervals a combined gas station and liquor store would float by in a halogen bubble, briefly commanding our attention like a television set flicked on in a dark room.

Ken — "the one hippie I won't get into a fight with," Ray called him — asked Ray about the punk band that he'd roadied for. Ray's stories always featured an adversarial redneck or two, a cool old black man, and some unlikely saviour, maybe a grizzled cop who collected obscure jazz records and rescued him and the band from a sticky situation. Travellers' stories. I'd hardly ever been outside of Toronto, but I knew Ray's stories well enough to punctuate them with asides, elaborations, and in-jokes.

Danny mocked us from the back. "Listen to the Toronto comedians, eh, trying out their new routine."

"Oh Dad, be quiet," Ray said, transforming Danny into the uptight father at a mobile sleepover party and the rest of us into kids stifling giggles when a parent shouted, "Don't make me come up there!" Danny, trying to wrest some dignity from this dynamic, propped himself up on one elbow and said, "Yeah, I used to go out to the islands with these guys. They weren't a band, but they used to go to all the happenings." I could hear the wind whistling up from the rust holes in the floor of Danny's home. No one said anything. We were waiting for him to spew his nostalgia, to remind us how everything was better in the '60s and '70s, how it all *meant* something back then. We'd wait until Danny fell asleep and then we'd laugh at him and tell our own stories, stories that would be a spell against ever ending up like the old hippie sleeping on the floor.

"We ran into these bikers one time," Danny said. "We were all camping in the woods and these bikers showed up saying they wanted to party. You had to let bikers party with you. They beat the fuck out of a bunch of the guys, then they raped the women."

The quiet in the van grew more self-conscious, as if we are all willing each other not to speak. Danny was in danger of turning into a tragic figure, a transformation none of us was ready for.

Danny said, "I hid in the woods. Had to get away, eh."

Ray actually looked over at me and frowned, knowing what a sucker I am for a sad story. Ray would talk to me about it later, he would concede that, yes, Danny had been through some bad shit. But don't talk now, Ray was telling me. Everyone will be a little nicer to Danny in the morning, he was telling me, that's the best we can do.

When we were finally on the right eastbound highway, Ken took my place in the passenger seat and I settled between them. Everyone else was asleep. It was almost dawn, and rock formations the size of apartment buildings began to appear on either side of the road. We began to pass a joint back and forth. Back in Toronto, "Hacky Sack" and "patchouli" and any other words associated with hippies were automatically as laugh-inducing as speaking in an exaggerated German accent, but Danny excepted, Ray and I were getting along with the hippies. Ken began to tell Ray about the barter fair, how everyone there was trying to "get off the grid" by bartering what they made or grew.

"I see it like this," Ken said, "a bunch of people could get some land up around Alaska — it's practically free under the Homesteader's Act. We would put up cabins and waxworks and ironworks and stoneworks, so that all the North

American gypsies like us would have a place to make their crafts in the winter."

When we were alone Ray would mock Ken's idealism, but for now he was gracious and attentive, like a father listening to a child's plan for a go-kart with amphibious wheels and retractable wings.

The campsite was set on a plateau against the side of a low, crumbling mountain. It was the only flat land around. The yellow grass and patches of trees rolled off in uneven waves toward the mountains in the west and prairies in the east, giving the place the feel of a borderland. My first thought when I stumbled out of the van was that the site was a pioneer homestead abandoned in impossibly tragic circumstances by the family that had broken their bodies clearing the rocks and trees.

A kind of oval roadway had been mowed through the grass, with cars and vans and buses tightly parked all around it. I was lying in the grass outside the van while the younger hippies set up their tents. I hadn't thought about where Ray and I were going to sleep — in the van, probably.

Danny was talking to a hippie who'd wandered over to our site. The hippie was wearing a porkpie hat and old navy-blue worker's overalls and had a troubadour's goatee, but one look at him told me that he would tear me apart in a fight. His body bristled against the rustic outfit, like a pit bull struggling against a muzzle.

He asked Danny if he knew a guy named Ernie Low.

"I know Ernie Wild."

"What about Free?"

"Where's he from?"

"All over."

"No."

"What about Tripper John?"

His name was Sage. Sage, he told Danny, is a sacred plant burned in Native American ceremonies: "That's why I wear it in my hat." He bent his head to show us the sprig of sage in his hat. I was standing up by then. Sage shook my hand, a formality that set him even further apart from the other hippies I'd met.

"This is my new dog, Orbit," he said, introducing us to a lanky, short-haired dog that had Doberman in its genes. "We just found each other last night. Think we're going to hang out for awhile, aren't we, boy?" Sage patted the dog on its haunches. He knew how to handle dogs. "He's only about eight months old and look at the size of him."

Danny had remembered something. "Hey, did Tripper John ever live in Venice Beach?"

"Wouldn't surprise me."

"You ever been to L.A., man?"

Sage looked at me when he heard the name of the city. I could tell that he was appealing to me for something — sympathy or at least a fair hearing. Tough men have a habit of casting me in the role of sympathetic, sensitive younger brother. It's always been that way with me. I nodded to him. He said, "I lived there for three years after I got out of the Marines. I was a bill collector for a medical agency. Did it for almost two years." He let a long pause describe the kind of work he had done for the company. "Then one day I looked at the people around me — I mean *looked*. They all looked like a bunch of ghouls, vultures, and I asked myself, am I living or am I dead? So I went back to nature." He looked at Ken, who was standing beside me. "I haven't used money in years, just bartering. I make pipes."

All the hippies in our party had gathered around us. They all nodded at the story's coda. They said "cool" and "all right, brother."

Ray came back from the row of toilet sheds and the two of us began to explore. There didn't seem to be any organized bartering going on — no one had travelled by caravan to trade a season's harvest for bolts of cloth and spices and cooking pots. There was organic produce for "sale or barter," handcrafted pipes, drums, and silver jewellery laid out on blankets, with the odd keener standing behind a folding table displaying homemade soap or lumpy pottery. Massage tables were set up about every fifty feet, and a few professional flea-market vendors sold a hundred things made out of plastic and composite metals. The younger hippies strolled around looking over the stuff like party-goers checking out the host's bookshelves and record collection, pausing to touch something they coveted but rarely asking how much it cost. Their bodies displayed patches of Lollapalooza paganism — piercings and vaguely Oriental tattoos — and they'd replaced 1960s' tie-dye with Mayan and Inca peasant wear, but otherwise the young hip-pies were doing a cover version of another generation's anthem.

Within an hour Ray had divided the campers into three categories: weekenders, freaks, and real people, the first cat-egory outnumbering the other two by a wide margin. We retreated into our private world of in-jokes and nasty asides. Ray stopped in front of a canvas teepee as white as a sail with some kind of bird painted over the entrance: "You think there's any Indians in there?"

"Jungians, maybe."

"Good one."

I went off on a rant about indigenous cultural appropria-tion, which Ray met with a tolerant expression I was well used to. "Yeah," he said, "it's all just recycled '60s' bullshit."

"You can't find yourself when you're stoned all the time," I said.

"You can't find your shoes when you're high all the time."

A lot of people wanted to barter for the beer Ray and I had smuggled into the camp in violation of the "NO ALCOHOL OR FIREARMS" sign at the gate. We traded cans of beer for food, two thick undershirts, and a set of coasters. After trading eight beers for two grams of mushrooms, we traded for just about anything — little wizards carved out of driftwood, packs of damp incense, a deck of nudie cards with a Queen of Hearts who Ray insisted looked exactly like his favourite high-school teacher. It didn't matter if she really did or not, it was a funny story.

We wandered off into the pine woods, climbing a hill that took to us to a small ridge where a few trees had been cleared. The cool air and the setting sun and the mushrooms made the sky look like a giant dome of overglazed pottery. If we climbed a little higher we could touch the base of the dome and feel ourselves safely encased in the valley. The sound of music and drum beats drifted up from the camp-site, then disappeared when the wind shifted.

Ray opened two beers. "You can drink this American stuff all night."

"Man, that Darlene," I said.

"Ah fuck, I knew it."

"No, man, she's so, I don't know — like open-hearted or focussed or something."

"You're just horny. Don't cloak your bestial urges in noble peasant cloth, my friend."

We laughed for at least a minute.

"What does that mean?" I asked.

"I don't know, but it's the most genius thing I've ever said.

I am so fucking high!"

We drank the beers. I had to say it: "Man, that fucking story Danny told last night, eh."

"Jesus. Man. Of course he did run away and hide in the bushes while everyone was getting stomped."

"What would you have done?"

"Not been there in the first place. What were they thinking? I mean, *fuck*."

"Bikers wouldn't have laid a hand on that Sage guy."

"They'd have invited him to join the club. He's one of those guys who knows how to kill a man with his toenails. Wonder how long it will take for him to crack up?"

"He's got a dog to hang out with," I said. "That helps."

"I remember my dad would go up to any dog and pet it and grab its fucking jaws and shake it. I thought he was going to get his fucking hand bitten off but he never did."

"My dad loved dogs but he hated cats," I said, just remembering this. "They totally spooked him. He could watch two dogs fighting or a dog trying to kill a squirrel and he would just smile, like everything was all right in the world. But cats — he used to say that cats were different, they killed for pleasure, it was like a blood fever came over them. It's like my dad believed that violence was okay for dogs because it was violence committed for honour, violence for food or loyalty, violence for territory. Cats just got off on killing. He couldn't handle that."

"I can see that," Ray said. "Sometimes I think we live in a world where dog violence is the only thing protecting us from cat violence. Barely."

Down at the site we started sharing our second case of beer with anyone who made it onto Ray's list of "real people." A guy who lived in a trailer and made jewellery, hearing that

we were Canadian, told tender stories illustrating Neil
Young's influence on his life. Around one of the communal
campfires, two ex-therapists joked about their former
clients. A woman and her husband explained a system they'd
developed for getting their goats in faster at the end of the
day. The people around the fire wore plain, faded clothes
over their faded skin and had home-cut hair. Their arms
were tightly wound rope and their midsections shaped like
feed bags. Something had been broken and remade in every
one of them, and in the firelight you could catch their
former identities asserting themselves in ghost gestures: a
sudden hand movement acquired in boardroom deal-
making sessions, a batting of the eyes that was once a signal
for flirtation — the fading accents of pioneers abandoning
their mother tongue. One of the ex-therapists would rest his
chin in his right hand about every ten minutes — the pro-
fessional's pose of thoughtful introspection — but he'd shoo
the affectation away by squeezing his jaw.

Some people were just broken. We met a bearded man in
a brown corduroy jacket and David-Crosby hat who
marched a tight circle around his ex-wife's car, stalking her
like a Greek chorus lamenting everything from their failed
marriage to the death of the counterculture.

"My woman," he cooed, "she's still into that Tom-
Robbins rainbow bullshit because she can't accept the
responsibilities of motherhood."

Both of them had been beautiful once, you could see it in
their skinny, faerie-faced children. She had driven the kids
to the fair from Seattle, hoping to sell enough of her belong-
ings to make it to L.A. where some unspoken salvation
waited for her.

Her possessions were laid out in neat rows on a blanket in
front of the car. There were scuffed beauty products and
hair clips, broken toys, radios, and mounds of clothing, all

arranged in seemingly patterned lines, like the verses of a cyclical poem recorded in pictographs.

"You didn't even bring a tent," he said.

"You can't keep a fucking job," she said.

Someone told us that there was going to be a drum circle later that night. That was too much for Ray. He got very quiet, not rising to any of the jokes I dangled for him. He said, "A *drum circle*, man, they're setting up a fucking drum circle." He was working himself into a state, chewing those words — drum circle — as if they contained the bitterness of everything that was wrong in the world. Ray could get that way. He'd see something that epitomized pettiness and inauthenticity — some idiot saying racist things in a bar or a poser who made the mistake of liking one of Ray's favourite bands — and he'd stare in silence at the thing that enraged him, lost in bitter memories of his hometown, where he'd played the role of the token freak of his high school. Then he'd sneer and nod compulsively, muttering affirmations to himself, as if he were hearing a voice from his past mocking him, only now he was too grown up to believe what the voice was saying but not wise enough to stop listening.

Almost everyone in the camp had started heading toward a dome of orange light and shadow flickering against the side of a steep hill just outside the ring of cars and campers and tents. A few bongo drums were shepherding beats around a simple, mid-tempo heartbeat. Ray and I began to walk to the drum circle. I didn't want to go, but Ray was liable to pick a fight or throw a full can of beer or a handful of rocks at someone.

"Haven't I seen all this before?" I said.

"Yeah, Woodstock the movie."

Ray and I started to race up a hill that ran to the left of what looked like a huge bonfire. We were having a race, throwing punches where we could see each other running in the dark. When was the last time I'd actually raced anyone? We were giggling and trying to trip each other, ruts and little rises nipping at our ankles, and when I got ahead Ray tackled me from behind. He made it to the top of the hill first and stood there, his still body a dramatic silhouette, an ancient standing stone watching from the dark hilltop. I stood beside him and looked down on about two hundred people shuffling around a bonfire that Ray estimated was the "size of a cottage." The sight of the flames was enough to sluice the rest of Ray's anger into a few cracks about the unoriginality of the hippies as they danced and clapped and played drums. A few of the men danced naked, but none of the women went further than stripping down to their skirts and bras. I looked for Darlene in the crowd and was grateful not to see her, knowing that I would have gone down there if I had.

"You're all going back to fucking work on Monday," Ray yelled.

The fire dancers were willing themselves into trances. They described shapes in the air with their hands — curves and circles and spirals. One dancer threw back his head and yelled at the sky. The rest of the dancers liked that — they howled too. I saw the Neil Young fan standing to the side, quietly smiling to himself and keeping time with his feet. One of the ex-therapists was dancing naked, warming his white hairy belly before the fire. And there was poor Danny, blowing a huge joint and duck-walking inside the circle. He handed the joint to someone and pulled a harmonica out of his back pocket and began to play badly.

I said to Ray, "Where do they go from here?"

"Fuck, home to the suburbs?"

"No, I mean, okay, you're here, you're naked and you're

dancing around a fire. I mean, where do you *go* from here?"

I couldn't describe what I was trying to get at. I lay down on the grass and looked up at all the stars I couldn't see in the city. The fire was so high that even on the hill we felt blasts of heat, like when my mother would open the oven door when I was a kid hanging around the kitchen. The blast of heat that smells like dinner.

THE GOVERNMENT OF THE SPIDERS

Like many of David's clients, the Norris family had knocked down most of the walls on the main floor of their Victorian row house, replacing the pannelled, closed rooms and hallway with an open living space. The rooms were still implied — two couches made a viewing gallery around a flat-screened TV, and there was a certain gravity to the dining-room set that discouraged the transfer of snacks from oak table to green couch — but the total effect suggested a concourse of light and air. David was standing by the dining-room table. He looked up and wondered why the unsupported ceiling didn't cave in on him. He couldn't find any pillars. Someone had thought all of this through.

Ken Norris was whistling in the kitchen, which was cut off from the main room by a tiled breakfast counter dusted with toast crumbs that David would have to clean up later. Ken wore comfortable black pants and a white University of Toronto sweatshirt that hung on a neck and shoulders as elegantly sloped as an expensive coat hanger. Years of physical labour had bulked up asymmetrical muscle groupings over David's bones, leaving him with a strong but constantly aching body shaped like a rolled-up futon mattress left to stand in a corner. David was strong enough to kill Ken and take everything he owned. Instead he was cleaning his house. It was the riddle of the ages. It was as if they had signed a compact, long before either could hold a pen, that decreed that Ken would grow up to be a lawyer and David a house cleaner.

David had tried to explain this to Janet, but she said, "You don't even believe that." He said, "I know, it's all my fault." He couldn't tell her that he felt as if he'd been walking through a room stuffed with invisible pillows since he'd graduated from art school. Janet didn't go for similes — things were never like any other thing but themselves.

Ken walked out of the kitchen and caught David staring at him. He smiled at David, pretending that they were playing a familiar game. On this bright winter morning the main room looked like an atrium in a much warmer country. Ken stepped into a shaft of light and said, "Alison and Emma went to the drop-in centre a little early this morning. You just missed them."

"No one has to be here," David said. "You can leave me a key and I'll slip it through the mail slot when I leave." David was now standing close enough to Ken to see that there were no grease stains on his white sweat shirt, though he'd been frying bacon. Ken hadn't been wearing an apron. Men like Ken didn't wear aprons, even ones with "#1 DAD" written on them. Ken just willed the spitting grease away from his white shirt. They were fire-walkers, these people, they could stand before vats of spitting grease or tomato sauce and go unstained.

"I'll be in my upstairs office for a couple of hours today."

Ken walked by David and remembered something he was supposed to tell him — something about David helping himself to something to drink — and tried to say it through a mouth full of chewed muffin. A few crumbs dribbled down his chin, and he jerked his arm to rescue them before they tumbled to the floor. He laughed, spraying more crumbs, and because he was confident with the gesture, David laughed too.

"Look at me," Ken said. There was a spring in his step as he started up the staircase, as if he'd accomplished his task and a little more.

David watched him bound up the stairs. Ken had every right to be happy — he had finally found his comfort level with the cleaner. It was a predictable process, repeated at some point in every client's home like an obscure ceremony between the lord of the manor and his tenants. During the first few cleans, the client's demeanour veered wildly between extremes of politeness and forced jocularity. They had yet to choose a role to play: host, friend, boss. Then one day the client spoke to the cleaner with a full mouth or made a catty stab at someone who'd just been on the phone, and suddenly a safe passage between two worlds opened. Over the next few visits clients would linger near the cleaner experimenting with other unguarded moments, maybe even going so far as to establish in-jokes. Eventually this series of intimacies mystically absorbed the cleaner into the family, not as a child or sibling or parent, but a distant but welcome cousin who helped out around the house.

David wished he could meet Ken's joy. He wished he was more magnanimous, but his natural response was to match Ken's intimacy with one of his own, which was against the rules of the ceremony.

David brought his unbleached rags into the kitchen and went to the cupboard beneath the sink where the environmentally friendly cleaning detergents were stored. In the sink was a round, flat, grease-clotted filtering devise with a black handle. David stared at it while he wet one of the rags, deciding that the device must be a specialized crepe-making accessory for a frying pan. He had never eaten crepes.

David started to clean the kitchen, though he should have

started on the third floor because dust, once disturbed, always settles on a lower surface. A cleaner dusts the highest surface first and works their way down. It was all in the manual. But Ken was up in his office. He would leave the room if asked, or just tell David to skip the office for one week — but either option entailed conversation. David couldn't bear the thought of talking to Ken, especially now that Ken felt comfortable enough to make small talk. Ken might even ask David a few questions about himself.

An hour later the main floor and all of the second floor save for the bathroom were clean. David was sitting in the kitchen about to eat his morning snack, an oversized choco-late-chip cookie. There was evidence of the Norris' son on the fridge: a team hockey photo, an ultraviolent drawing, a maudlin Mother's Day card that seemed to show a plump woman made out of tropical fruit.

David broke his cookie into eight roughly equal pieces, seven of which he put back into the waxpaper. He ate the first piece and reached into the waxpaper to grab a second when Ken walked into the kitchen carrying an empty coffee cup. His eyes flickered from the waxpaper and the cookie fragment in David's hand up to the cupboard where a bag of the same brand of cookies was kept. David's hand froze a few inches from his mouth. Initiating a conversation about cookies would force David to explain why he had broken the cookie into eight equal pieces and hidden seven of the pieces away. Why had he concealed the uneaten pieces?

He and Ken began to exchange a series of highly ritual-ized twitches — not unlike those of two male insects confronting each other on opposing journeys along a twig — that if converted into language would have read:

I can't believe you stole a fucking cookie.

You said I could help myself.

To something to drink!

I'm sorry, I misunderstood.
I'll give you the benefit of the doubt this time.
Don't do me any favours.
Thief.
Prick.

Clients can overlook a stray dust-bunny under a dresser, but not cleaning the toilet properly would be worse than serving a meal on dirty dishes. And as David's boss pointed out, a client would never complain if the seat or bowl is dirty, as doing so would incriminate them as the source of the embarrassing stains.

"A spotless bathroom is the signature on the contract between client and cleaner," David's boss said.

"You should make a sign," David said.

David was cleaning the Norris toilet wondering if he'd locked the bathroom door. Worse than doing a bad job on the toilet would be the client actually seeing David at the job. It was fine, even recommended, to leave the door open when scrubbing the tub, but the door was to be closed and locked when tackling the toilet. "The client has to believe that the toilet cleans itself," went the frameable golden rule. It was a good rule, because if violated the entire capitalist apparatus would be stripped down to its most basic template, a zoological chart mapping the hierarchy of sentient, money-earning life. Somewhere in the middle of this chart would be Ken Norris, represented in icon as a pair of four-hundred-dollar reading glasses and Saturday *New York Times*, while lower on the chart scuttled David, a half-savage kneeling reverently before a toilet.

The toilet seat was stained with flashes of electric-yellow urine, the afterbirth of too many vitamin supplements. David imagined good health as a measurable element, like gold, and men like Ken pissing their excess down the toilet. David looked up at the door again. The door knob was secured by pushing and turning the knob like the lid of a childproof aspirin bottle. He would have remembered locking it.

David did remember reminding himself to lock the bathroom door as he walked up the stairs, but a fantasy had descended on his intention, leaving a memory white-out between the staircase and the toilet. Like all of his fantasies, it lacked a narrative structure. The fantasy consisted of David kneeling before Alison Norris. She was naked and he had his arms wrapped around her knees and his chin buried against her firm lower abdomen. Looking up, the rises of her ribs and breasts were a horizon that, like mountains in the distance, never seemed to get closer.

Alison was a variation of the archetypal woman he'd wanted to marry since he was four years old. Straight butterscotch-brown hair, big eyes, clear but lightly weathered skin, and high cheekbones. Her comfortable but not frumpy clothes were clean, slightly faded, and worn in the right places — no threadbare patches at the knees or cuffs to hint at manual labour or a modest clothing budget. And her personality — the totality of which he saw as a wheel of expensive pre-sliced Brie — was neatly apportioned, some wedges devoted to her children, others to appreciating art and friends and what sophisticated Europeans in movies enthusiastically referred to as *life*, while still other wedges served her career goals. At the centre of this wheel, wrapped in red cellophane and flavoured with herbs that grew only by moonlight, lay her *mysterious core*. On nights calculated by celestial correspondences, she unwrapped the red cellophane and ate of herself and gave of herself to her lover, closing the wrapper at night's end knowing the core would be replenished.

Pushing the fantasy forward, Alison would have crooked her hand in David's armpit and pulled him up to face her. "Here is what I want you to do," she would have said, and like a lady-in-waiting sending her chaste knight out to slay the local tyrant, Alison would have counselled him to parlay his talents — he was an artist, he was good with computers — into the down payment on a downtown Victorian house worthy of her patronage.

David heard a muffled step in the hall. It was too late to jump up and lock the door, so he reached instead for his bottle of spray-cleaner and pointed it at the door like a gun. The door swung open and Alison stepped into the bathroom carrying two mugs on a cocktail-waitress tray. David was caught, down on his knees looking up at Alison. The brown cocktail tray she carried was made of hard plastic and cork board. Frayed tassels of a promotional beer sticker clung to the lip of the tray. He recognized the make of tray from his art-school days when he had worked as a busser in a pseudo-English pub. Alison must have stolen the tray from a bar where she had worked as a waitress, in a life before careers, and children, and Ken. Her life would have been all potential then: school not over, a career not quite chosen, Ken just one of the men she shared her futon with.

David felt his heart break, knowing that for a brief window of time he could have legitimately asked Alison out on a date. They could have fallen in love and shared a path into the future, and that future would be now, and she would be bringing him coffee in his office, not here in the bathroom but upstairs where he would be hard at work on an important project. And she would ask him about the project, and he would complain about the client, and she would laugh knowingly. Then he would put his work aside and ask about her client, and she would complain, and they would laugh knowingly. *Clients*, they'd say.

Alison looked into the toilet bowl, which was crowded with won-tons of toilet paper that he'd been using to clean the seat, though the company handbook prescribed bleach-free cloth rags for the job. The shock of finding David cleaning the family toilet seemed to temporarily numb the muscles in Alison's face, forcing her to reach into an emergency stash of stock expressions and making do with the closest available, that of the nine-year-old who has barged in on her parents fucking.

"I should have knocked," she said.

"No, it's . . ."

"I *really* should have knocked. You could have been in the bathroom." She laughed, her way of saying, "You know what I mean."

"I would have locked the door," he said. He stood up and stripped off his rubber gloves. He wanted to explain to her that he had dropped a valuable ring, an heirloom of his once-noble family, into the toilet, where it lay under the man-of-war of toilet paper wads. His hands flexed, grasping for a hold in the air, something solid, a tool to turn the ship of his future around. His hands, he realized, were flexing at the air for some *work*, for a job to do, as any working man's hands do when faced with a problem.

"I brought you coffee." She put the tray on the laundry hamper and handed a mug to David, who took the mug in one hand before she could turn the handle toward his fingers. He looked down at the mug, the damp protecting his palm from the worst of the heat.

"You're burning yourself," she said.

"I've got callouses." It was beginning to hurt. David couldn't let her know that it hurt.

She looked at his unscathed hand, the fingers glowing pink, as if a bright light were shining inside the mug. They looked at each other, and he saw for the first time that there were crow's feet around her eyes and a smudge of bright children's food on her shirt. Before her children were born Alison had worked for a design firm. She had set up a home office a few months earlier, a small bedroom that, judging by a scuffed border of wallpaper dolls, had been the children's nursery. A two-month-old *People* magazine was draped over a pile of papers on the drafting table. There were quartz bookends carved in the shape of Central American religious figures on a spare dresser, herding about a dozen trade paperbacks into a slouching row: *The Tibetan Book of Living and Dying*, Jung's *Man and His Symbols*, something by the Dalai Lama.

Alison was staring at his bright red hand still holding the coffee mug. She looked amazed but a little skeptical, as if she were torn between believing that David possessed miraculous powers or was performing a common magic trick. Alison reached out to touch his hand, but David, almost crying from the pain, put the mug in the sink, spilling some of the coffee.

She pulled away, shocked. "Your hand. You've burned it."

"No."

"I've hurt you."

"It doesn't hurt."

"It must hurt."

"This is my painting hand," he said. Technically, this was true. "I used to get blisters. They became callouses."

"I used to get a terrible callous on this finger," she said. She was looking at his arms, at the veins and muscles raised by scrubbing the bath and the toilet.

From downstairs Emma called, "Mommy, the letter song!"

"Emma's watching *her show*."

"Yes," he said.

Emma called again from downstairs.

"I'd better see what she wants. I'm sorry about your hand."

"It's fine."

She smiled. "Good," she said. "There's juice and water downstairs. It gets so dry in here."

He closed the door and leaned against it, following the sounds of her footsteps. He realized that his heart was pounding, his mouth dry. Was that why she said it gets so dry in here? He walked over to the medicine cabinet, a doorless trio of shelves set into the wall to the right of the sink. He wanted ointment for his hand, his hand that, for relief of a little bit of pain, had betrayed him when he needed it most. If he could have held onto the mug a little longer, Alison might have touched him.

Sitting on one of the shelves was the small vial of prescription pills that had been there since last week. Cleaning houses is like walking through a life-size connect-the-dots puzzle: the cleaner sees the numbers that delineate their client's lives, but decorum demands they not connect them. He had seen the vial last week, but the label had faced the wall. Nothing could have compelled him to turn the label and read it, but today the label faced out. The prescription was for A. Norris. Proval: an aerodynamic name, affirmative, the hip grandchild of all those Greek and Latin syllable chains. Take one pill in the morning with lots of water.

David read the whole label without touching the vial. He opened the vial. The pill was sour and chalky. He put six in a wad of dry toilet paper, which he shoved into his pocket.

Janet was a nurse. She and David had been living together for almost four years. David assumed that they were saving for a house, and that he wasn't keeping up his end of that bargain very well. Janet often told him that he should take his boss up on her unspoken but hinted offer to come in as a partner in the cleaning business.

"But that would give me less time to paint," he'd argue.

"You haven't started a painting for months."

"I know, I already have so little time."

That night at dinner David asked Janet what Proval was.

"Proval is the newest antidepressant on the block — and it's very expensive." Janet specialized in second-guessing careless doctors on their prescription choices for patients on her ward. "It makes your mouth really dry, but that seems to be the only side effect, besides the one-in-ten-thousand chance of total psychosis. Are you considering going on it?"

He was genuinely offended at the question. "No, this guy I know is on it."

"Who?" Janet knew his few friends.

"This guy I knew in art school."

"And he told you he was on Proval?"

"He's one of those people who tells you details about his life you really don't want to know. He's living with this woman in her fifties who runs a gallery on Spadina."

"Is he going to have a show soon?"

"Of course he is, he's sleeping with the gallery owner. Never mind that his art sucks."

"Here it comes."

"What?"

"Forget it."

"No."

"Maybe you just don't like his art."

"No, it sucks."

"That's your opinion."

"That's my evaluation based on certain aesthetic criteria. Like has he any understanding of brush technique? Can he represent perspective and shading? Has he ever had an original idea in his life? No no no!"

"I guess he wouldn't be allowed into The Citadel."

"Fuck, I should never have told you about that." The Citadel was the utopian state he had formulated in the days when they used to get high together and talk for hours after sex. The Citadel was divided into farmers and artists and philosophers. The men did two years service in the army to toughen up; women on their periods went into communal huts to talk with the gods.

"Maybe you don't get what he's trying to do in his art."

"I get what he's trying to do — the operative word being *trying* — and I see that he's failed."

Janet put her knife and fork down. "Why do you act like any artist whose work you don't like has personally insulted you or fucked your mother or something?"

"No one fucks my mother! Not even my dad."

For the first few days on the medication David experienced his usual range of emotions — negative, defensive, fleeting — but his attitude toward them quickly changed. The fact that he *had* an attitude to them was proof of transformation, for David had never been anything but the current sum of his emotions. Now he was David Being Critical of His Girlfriend, now he was David Totally Likes This Reggae Song, now he was David Had Too Many Carbohydrates with Lunch. Within three days the medication had narcoticized this protean self, encasing it in a bubble of what felt like static electricity, leaving a reborn David standing safely outside that bubble. The new David experienced the old David as a kind of unpleasant itch, like a bone mending in the front of his skull. The new David stood alone on a clean plane of silence, and he filled the silence of his Garden with a stream of mesmerizing self-affirmations, the first of which bore all the others on its mighty back: David deserved to be as happy as anybody else. It was obvious. Why shouldn't he be happy? Why not he, *David*?

So David knew what he would say when Alison confronted him about the missing pills. The effect of the pills provided the defence for the crime: David would deny the theft of the medication by saying that it wasn't theft because he deserved the pills.

David was also sure that Alison wouldn't confront him. Like a murderer who leaves a clue in hope of being caught, Alison had wanted him to find those pills. On the way over to the Norris' that Monday morning he imagined another bathroom meeting with Alison in which he'd admit to stealing her medication.

I know I shouldn't have —
No, that's why I left them out for you —
I should have at least —
It had to be this way —
I tried to —
How could I have possibly told you?
It's so beautiful now.
Yes.

But standing now before the Norris house David was overcome by an updraft of weightlessness, a rapidly ascending fizz of doubt that evaporated his feet, calves, testicles, and nipples. Ringing the doorbell restored his torso.

Alison swung open the door.

David said, "Good morning!"

"Good morning to you, sir."

"How are you today?"

"Up and down."

They fired these lines at each other at a level of volume and emotional neutrality clearly meant to be overheard and registered as common conversation. David was sure that she hadn't blinked yet. He was expecting her to silently mouth,

"There's a man in the kitchen with a gun." She wouldn't look him in the eye, but she didn't seem to be in a hurry to rush past him or retreat into the house. Emma was already dressed for the outdoors. She hid behind Alison's legs.

"Emma wanted to tell you that the bucket and mop are in the basement."

"Thank you, Emma," he said. "I would have been looking for them all morning."

Then, remembering something very important and proud to have remembered it, Emma told him to be careful of the basement stairs. "The government of the spiders," she said, looking up at her mother for confirmation. "The government of the spiders lives under the stairs."

"Yes, there's a government under my stairs at home," David said. "But he keeps the flies away."

"But he might jump out at you — for true."

"I'll be careful."

Alison smiled at his sensitivity. If an atom bomb were detonated at that moment they'd be vapourized in this family pose into the foundation wall for the edification of future archaeologists.

"Emma starts nursery school today," Alison said in a voice that cast David as audience and ally. "Monday, Wednesday, Friday mornings, right, honey?"

"No!"

"Mommy needs to get some work done. You'll have lots of fun work to do, honey."

David felt his feet evaporating again. "Will I be letting myself in, then?"

Alison looked him in the eye now. "I'll be working in my office upstairs." The direct statement seemed to drain her. "Daddy's going to be working at his *office* office, right, honey?"

Emma looked up, confused. She was losing track of the

rules of this word game. "Mommy's starting a business," she said.

"That's right." Alison put on her coat and mouthed a goodbye and left.

David tried to add up the signals Alison and Emma had sent him. Emma was off to daycare. Alison was working at home. Ken was working at his firm's office. The government of the spiders was in the basement.

He opened the basement door. The stairs shifted and mumbled in their sleep as he descended and groped the unshaven brick wall in search of a light switch. To his right was a sheer drop into dark storage. Ahead, light pooled beneath a small window half-buried in snow. The sudden sharpening of the smell of dust told him that he had passed below ground level. At the bottom of the stairs he turned and did a slow shuffle into the darkness, scooping the air for hanging strings or bare lightbulbs. He could have found a light switch with his eyes closed in any living room or bedroom in the city, but the wiring in basements followed no pattern. Unless converted to revenue-generating apartments, his clients' basements were a mess. Gone were the basement playrooms of his childhood, the ping-pong tables and workshops, the stand-up bars festooned with British pub mats and tit-shaped ice-cube moulds and packets of calcified Tom Collins mix. David's clients only had enough life and time to fill up two floors. They lacked imagination.

By the time his knees bumped into what was either a clothes dryer or a storage freezer, David had converted the room into a basement studio that maximized the natural light from the windows he would install while playfully incorporating the room's inevitable trellis work of ducts and wires. He groped along the wall and found a light switch. A washer and dryer were pushed into a corner. The washer's front panel had been removed and was leaning against the wall, exposing the machine's black tubes, one of which arced up and out from the round tub, a thick rubber protuberance that made David think of a 19th-century feminine-hygiene apparatus stored far from the men's quarters. He knew, from a note on the fridge, that Alison was supposed to have called a man to fix the machine three weeks ago. A pile of clothes waited beside the laundry sink. On a drying rack Ken's dress shirts hung upside down in rows, the sheered forequarters of vaguely simian livestock left to drain and cure in the cool air.

David put his finger in the protruding tube. He touched one of the shirts that would never dry in the basement. He was meant to see this: the gutted symbol of domesticity Alison refused to repair, the shirts hanging in the damp air.

He stole seven more pills before he left.

Alison changed her life. She cleaned her office, sweeping the drafting table clean save for one sheet of oversized paper. Someone had the washing machine repaired, and the mountain of laundry in the basement seemed to have exploded into piles of colour-sorted magma that dwindled by the week. Ken and the kids were always gone by the time David arrived at nine on Monday mornings.

David also made changes. He started working on a few paintings, massive canvasses of yellow and orange that were pure emanation and heat and fertile passivity, visual dispatches from a pollen-gathering mission on the first morning of summer. He mixed drops of essential oil into the paint and didn't even get angry when Janet called his four-foot-by-six canvas "the world's largest scratch-and-sniff painting." He tried to explain to her that the painting was about an inner transformation he was experiencing, one that couldn't be captured in representational forms. She told him to stop talking in that creepy voice again. "You sound like the grown-up kids trying to be nice to their parents in the cancer ward," she said.

When Alison let David into the house on Monday mornings the air was mastered by the smell of sharp good coffee, undiluted by the lingering odours of bedrooms hastily vacated or toast scorched at the edges. The nerves on David's skin told him that Alison was alone in the house. The bright winter light made the main room throb, as if a great force were trying to rise from under the pine floorboards, then the room would go so silent and still that David would want to say something in a loud, clear voice, a proclamation in verse or a confession of guarded love in the quivering tones of an American actor in the climax of a romantic comedy. The reflected sunlight made a black outline around Alison's body so that she looked superimposed onto the scene from another, higher dimension. The black line was a set of illustrated instructions: cut along the line, remove Alison carefully, and transplant onto better life. David would try to think of the right thing to say to make this happen but Alison would turn away and tell him to help himself to water or juice or coffee — it was always dry in the house, she said. "You know where everything is," she said, evoking the vial of Proval, which hovered in the air between them like a cheap special effect symbolizing their clandestine union. That's how it was between them, then: they were forbidden lovers, each held captive in their ancestral manse, their astral bodies meeting at midnight in some ancient oak grove beyond the moons of Venus.

While he went around the house cleaning, Alison would sit in her office phoning people, reconnecting with an old network of friends and colleagues that must have been the centre of her life and work before her children were born. Once she had dispensed with the necessary milestones — yes, little Emma was in nursery school, yes, her son was quite the hockey player *and* good in math — her tone turned slightly sarcastic and confiding. She told anecdotes that showed her children to be demanding, slightly spoiled creatures, ultimately loveable in the end. Ken did not figure so well, appearing as a distracted father and husband from a 1950s' sitcom. It all sounded like gossip to David, but business must be conducted differently in Alison's world, where work was an extension of social networks. Alison couldn't just phone up old contacts and ask them for a freelance contract. There were no labour exchanges in her world, no men in peacoats waiting outside a heated trailer petitioning for a day's work. David was learning.

David found excuses to be near Alison while she talked, lingering outside her office, wiping phantom scuffs from the railings, or redusting the dresser next to her drafting table. He soon realized that she didn't mind him listening. She even began to provide him with a visual commentary on her phone calls, rolling her eyes when the person on the other end went on for too long and winking when her sarcasm went unheeded. Soon she began to mouth silent jokes to David, drawing him deeper into a conspiracy of ridicule. David had noticed that there was always a tall glass of water at her desk, so he began to bring her a fresh glass of water when the phone calls dragged on. She would nod thank you and touch his arm, making even the water a treasured secret between them. At the end of the morning, after cleaning the bathroom, David would steal seven more pills, elated that Alison was allowing him to continue, disappointed that she hadn't left him a note in the vial, a few words granting him permission to make the next move.

Then one morning when David went to the third floor to clean Ken's office, he heard someone speaking behind the half-closed door. It was an unfamiliar male voice. The speaker sounded angry, imperious, as if Ken was being dressed down by an angry client. Why hadn't Alison warned David not to go up to the third floor? Maybe she wanted David to hear Ken being humiliated, to demonstrate that Ken could be put in his place like anyone else. David leaned against the banister, willing himself to breathe normally. He heard what sounded like bubbles breaking on the surface of water. Someone called out: "I'm not getting any younger!" It was the voice of the modern movie villain — slightly shrill, psychotically self-assured, dispatching good guys with corny tag lines and bad puns.

"I don't have all day!"

David pushed open the door.

"Excuse me, I'm in the middle of an adventure here."

Ken's computer was turned up loud. Someone, probably the son David had never met, had been interrupted in the middle of a video game, leaving a pirate stranded in a cave. The cartoon pirate stood next to a treasure chest, water dripping from the stalagmites above him and bubbling up from an infernal spring at his feet. There was a green parrot on his shoulder, and he tapped his one good leg against the cave floor.

"I'm growing impatient!"

David considered shutting the computer off. If it stayed on all day the silhouette of an impatient pirate might be permanently burned on the screen, but Ken might suspect nefarious intentions if David touched the computer. David left the computer alone. He walked out of the room, the pirate demanding that he continue the game.

David walked to Alison's office and stood watching her talk on the phone. She looked at him and smiled and continued complaining about Ken. "Yeah, yeah," she said, "I'll be a good wifey and make some sandwiches for you and the boys. I said that — half-joking of course — but Lawyer-Boy held me to the letter of the law later. *In front of my colleagues!*

he said. Have to keep up the professional veneer even when they're grunting over a hockey game." There was a long pause during which Alison shepherded the speaker's monologue forward with frequent *uh-huhs*, then she broke out laughing, holding the phone away from her mouth, well-mannered even in mirth. Another series of uh-huhs began, and she looked at David and transformed her hand into a puppet pantomiming logorrhea.

David left and returned with two glasses of water. He put one glass down in front of Alison. She nodded thank you. David stood before Alison in front of the chair. She looked up at him, letting the mouthpiece fall limp below her chin. He silently toasted her, drinking his entire glass of water in three long gulps. Alison accepted the challenge, gulping her own water without pausing. She put the water down and looked at him. David whispered, "I'm going to clean the bathroom," and walked out of the room without looking back at her.

David went into the washroom and closed the door without locking it. He was trying to remember what he'd been thinking about when she'd walked in on him that day when everything had changed between them. He knew that he had imagined her naked — Alison had been standing before him naked. In the fantasy he was down on his knees, his face almost touching her smooth belly. He was looking up at her, waiting for her to lift him up to her level. David repeated the fantasy, only this time he stood up himself, without waiting for her to touch him. They were facing each other. He closed his eyes.

Soon he heard Alison walking down the hallway. She came into the bathroom with two cups of coffee on a tray and gave him one. He took the mug in his hand. The mug burned his hand but he did not let go. She reached out and touched his hand.

THE LONG SLIDE

"I'd really like to drink that coffee," David said, "but I'm really dehydrated."

Alison nodded, bringing her forehead down in the universal gesture of encouragement.

"I can't drink enough these days," he said, putting the mug down. "I'm always thirsty," he said. "Fucking pills." It was a relief to finally say the words. They had been sitting in a hollow in his cheek for so long that they fell out of his mouth like calcified pellets.

"Dry-mouth is better than being a drooling freak," Alison said, making a crazy face, a vaudeville comedian's impersonation of a lunatic. They started laughing.

"We can do anything," he said, "and in a court of law we'd be found guilty with an explanation."

Alison took him by the elbow and led him into the master bedroom, then pushed him onto the bed. He took her wrist but she nodded no. "Look," she said. She began to undress for him. She looked at his eyes to make sure that he was watching her body as it was revealed to him.

It began as larval sex, the coupling of two creatures blind and hungry, groping toward a more static identity. Later David would remember the room in near darkness, though the blinds were half-drawn and it was another bright winter morning. He would remember a dull honeyed light, a sort of cocoon that gradually enveloped them as they lay together in the middle of the bed. Could Alison see this cocoon? Yes, at least some version of it, because their faces were mirror images and David could see her marvelling at the light. A shared pressure animated their bodies, and they pressed closer, crushing the space between them, until, like all of nature's transformations, their larval stage ended with sound and fluids.

The room was uniformly lit. David looked over at Alison. Her skin was shining with risen blood and a fine sheen of sweat. There had surely been two births — it was time to try out their new bodies. Alison rolled to the edge of the bed and David flipped into the warm spot she left behind. He watched her take a tissue from the painted macaroni-and-popsicle-stick dispenser Emma had made her for Mother's Day and wipe herself between the legs. She held the clump of tissue over the waste basket, saw that David had emptied it earlier, and placed the tissue on the bedside table. Would he be expected to clean it up? The possibility welled up that at some critical moment in the sex act Alison might have branched off onto a different evolutionary path, emerging as a radically different subspecies of their shared genus, some barely recognizable cousin with proboscis that would poke David's eyes out if he tried to hold her close.

She stood up and jumped into a pair of clean pants. "We'll have to talk," she said.

"We could have a drink."

"That's how we got into this in the first place." She came over and closed his eyelids, finishing the gesture with two kisses in place of pennies. "I haven't kissed your eyes yet. Can't forget to kiss your eyes."

He let go of a long exhale.

"You're relaxed," she said.

"I'm paralysed."

"The black widow strikes again!"

Alison thought that David was playing a game, but he really couldn't move. He would have to tell Janet what he'd done. She would leave him — he wouldn't respect her if she didn't. The separation would be clean and painful. After that? "Would you have slept with me if I didn't clean your house?" he asked Alison.

"No, it was the way you hold your spray bottle that attracted me."

"Really, if I was a doctor or a —" (not *lawyer*, don't bring *him* into it) "someone from your old design firm. Would you?"

"Come on, David. We'll have to talk. This was crazy. But you fucked me proper." She laughed. "A guy once propositioned me with that line: Alison, I'll fuck you proper."

"What are you going to do?" he asked.

"Eat lunch."

"I mean, in the big picture?"

"I don't know what you want me to say, David."

That he was her first lover since Ken. He wanted her to say that he was the new man in her life.

"David, please get up." Her voice seemed to be rising a half-scale with every reasonable sentence, climbing from husky intimacy to everyday weariness.

"I can't."

"David."

"Don't fucking touch me!" He pulled the blankets over his head. He was the child in a dream hiding in plain sight from the monster, believing that if he just closed his eyes and held his breath the monster would pass him by. Ken was a reasonable man. No scenes for Ken, just a simple accounting of the new situation — David in bed with his wife. Ken would pack his bags and file his papers, in that order. David would take up his boss on her offer to become a partner, work on his paintings in the evening, and step by rational step take his place in the human hierarchy next to Alison.

"David, talk to me."

"Leave me alone." He wasn't going anywhere until he was her husband.

"David, I haven't mislead you. It's not like I just . . ."

There — he was her first lover since Ken. There was a crack in the rock of Alison's life and the sex they had just had was the wet sliver of wood that would split the rock of her heart in two. He just had to wait it out.

Alison must have been wringing her hands by then. She gave David a time and place where they could meet: 4:30 on Saturday, at one of the Italian places on College. She reasoned, she begged, she scolded and screamed, but he wouldn't leave — he had just arrived for God's sake. She finally closed the bedroom door, leaving him alone in his Garden beneath the sheets.

Eventually Ken came home, mumbled incredulously in various rooms out of earshot of the children, then swung the bedroom door open and ripped the blanket off David. Ken's fists were clenched, but David's muscles and nothing-to-lose glaze kept Ken at bay. Ken sneered — he had other ways of getting David out of the bed.

Ken turned to the ghost called Alison. He told her that he was disappointed with her but not surprised. She had always loved drama, couldn't resist the grand gesture.

"That's right," he said, "blame it on the antidepressants."

Alison was in tears in under a minute. When she had keened "never ever again" the requisite number of times, they came together to devise a plan to get David out of the bed. Ken wanted direct action of some sort; Alison searched for footholds to help them climb the stone wall of David's psychosis. Ken signalled her to leave the room and they went downstairs.

Alone, David pulled the blanket over himself again. A TV came on somewhere in the house. It may have been a hallucination, but David saw Ken and the children appear as a single silhouette in the darkened bedroom doorway. Ken motioned the children to look at David, the dutiful father playing his role in a family ritual that might have been passed down to him from his father. *Look at the man on the bed, children. Look at the shame your mother has brought upon our house.*

Eventually two plainclothes detectives showed up. Ken

must have called in some pretty heavy favours to avoid the flashing lights in front of the house. One of the cops turned on the lights in the bedroom and asked Ken and Alison to wait downstairs.

"Get the fuck out of that bed," the bad cop said.

"I can't move."

"Now!"

They were both bad cops. One of them grabbed David by the balls and squeezed.

"Now!"

David was on College Street. He kept checking his zipper to make sure it was still done up. He imagined Ken and Janet as a married couple. It didn't work. They were too much alike — two hands that kept coming up "rock" in a game of paper-scissors-rock. David was tormented by scenes from the night he met Janet. He saw himself sitting on a bed in the emergency ward. He had tripped down a client's stairs and twisted his left ankle. He was sure his ankle was broken. Janet, a nurse on the ward, gently pressed on the elegant purple dome above his ankle and pronounced it sprained.

"Oh," he said, six weeks of paid leave slipping away.

"Sprained *badly*."

"Oh!"

"The doctor will tell you to stay off it."

As she was leaving he said, "Great uniform."

Janet turned around. "It brings out the blue in my veins, don't you think."

David smiled, knowing now that Janet wouldn't have made the joke without David's prompting and that he would have gone on believing his ankle was broken until a doctor finally told him otherwise.

That was all over.

Soon he was standing before a small fish store in Kensington Market, attracted by the garish sign painted on the front window. The picture depicted a large cartoon shark wearing a Hawaiian shirt. The shark stood erect on his tail fin holding a deep-sea fishing pole from which dangled a dripping fisherman. A pair of X's in place of eyes indicated that the fisherman was dead. The smiling shark winked. Behind the glass, rows of pink and silver ocean fish, their eyes glazed with a milky film, were stacked like firewood on a bed of ice. David followed the line of their tails toward the cash-register where an old man in a bloody apron rocked slowly on the balls of his feet, occasionally picking fish-scales from his wrist and then holding them up to the light. The old man stood in rapt attention contemplating the mystery of the fish scale. The scene took on the mystical symmetry of a Byzantine religious icon: Saint Vassily of the Fish Store. For a moment it seemed like the world would stay this quiet and pure forever, but then the old man scowled at David, and David, blushing past his hairline, began an elaborate series of hand gestures to indicate that he'd mistaken the fish store for — for what?

SOME KIND OF MORPHINE

It is the fourth anniversary of Karen's death. It's not like they're going to throw a memorial party, but Margaret tells Gavin that they should observe the date somehow.

"For Fiona's sake?" he asks.

"For Karen's sake," she says, her tone warning him not to make any bitter comments. Gavin hadn't been thinking about Karen that way, but he looks down into his tea, pretending that Margaret has just read his mind. If everyone insists on casting him as the bitter widower whenever Karen's name is mentioned he might as well take some pleasure in playing the role to its fullest. He's learned that there is no point arguing.

He and Margaret are sitting in the variety store/lunch counter that Fiona loves to come to on Saturday mornings for bacon and eggs. The old Greek couple who run the place call Fiona "Darling" and give her a free candy after breakfast. Margaret is on her lunch hour. She works at a woman's shelter south of King. "Why don't you come over after church tonight?" she says. "Tracy's coming over for dinner with Brian. She's just gotten back from Wilson."

Gavin would like to see Tracy and Brian. They finalize the plans, and when Margaret mentions church a second time Gavin realizes that she is telling him that he needs to be alone with his thoughts before he comes over. This is going too far, even by the rules Karen's death has imposed on them. Gavin wants to argue, tell Margaret that he's done almost nothing but be alone with his thoughts for the last five months. He barely thought about Karen in that time except to note how well Fiona has continued to deal with the absence of her mother. He's not saying that Fiona is better off without Karen, but he won't pretend that things haven't turned out pretty well.

Gavin keeps his mouth shut. People make him the bitter widower because they think that that's how they would feel in his place. Gavin has tried to explain this to Margaret, but he doesn't push. She was Karen's only sibling. She has been a second mother to Fiona. First, really.

Margaret must know that Gavin is pissed because she takes one of his hands and opens his clenched fingers to look at his palm. The last of his callouses are being reclaimed by the swirling patterns of skin. "Almost gone," she says.

"Girlie hands," he says, clenching.

"How is your back?"

"It's good."

"Don't overdo it," she says.

They look at each other and laugh. "Okay," he says. "I won't."

"Bring some dessert tonight." She stands up to leave.

"Don't you overdo it," he says, referring to the bulge in her stomach pushing against her loose shirt.

"Too late," she says. Her thoughts have already pushed ahead of the little smile on her face, sliding back into a familiar rut. There is another crisis at the shelter. One of the women went missing the night before. Margaret thinks she's gone back to the man who was beating her and forcing her to have sex with his friends for money. Margaret has seen it all — breakdowns, fights, overdoses, righteous pimps and husbands storming the front desk demanding their human property back. Margaret has started to wonder what all this stress might be doing to her unborn child. She says she has begun to resent the women's needs. She needs to protect herself from their problems. The professional distance between worker and client is no longer enough.

Gavin has his own ideas. No amount of money is worth what Margaret has to put up with. She should have quit years ago. She's done enough for other people — let her be selfish for a while. Look what happened to Karen, he wants to say. Everything started to go wrong when Karen got hired at the shelter. Gavin doesn't have a very good memory, especially about the order of events, but he remembers that Karen started to smoke a lot of pot a few weeks after she got the job. She told him that pot helped her relax, and he remembers how odd it was to hear Karen dividing her emotional states into "relaxed" and "tense."

Karen also got on that kick about her childhood about that time. She had never talked about anything that happened to her before the age of thirteen or so, even after Fiona was born. Then one day Karen told Gavin that she was never going to understand herself until she understood her childhood. One night while they were in bed she told Gavin that she had just remembered the most amazing thing: a nightmare that she had started having when she was six, the year her family moved to the suburbs. In the dream a man in a fedora and cape kidnapped her and locked her in the front room of his house while he went to eat dinner with his family. Karen waited at the door for the man to return. She was more curious than afraid. The room smelled like carpet cleaner. The couch and easy chair were covered in plastic. When the man returned he put Karen on the chair and started to touch her with his hands, which still smelled like his dinner: starchy potatoes and vinegar and some kind of fish. In the dream Karen would leave her body and fly up to the ceiling and look down on the man and the girl, who were doing something under the cape. Karen remembered feeling sorry for the girl, and also a little superior. The girl hadn't brought this on herself exactly, but she hadn't done much to prevent it either.

When Karen hit puberty the nightmare changed. The man would take her into the room but he wouldn't bother to eat his dinner. He was in a hurry. He was nervous about something. The man in the cape would start to touch her and just as Karen was about to leave her body another man would kick the door open. The man walked into the room and aimed a pistol at the man in the cape's head and fired. The man in the cape looked stunned as a tiny hole opened in his forehead. In the dream Karen could smell the blood pouring from his skull. The smell excited her. She wanted her rescuer to shoot the man in the cape again and again. She wanted him to shoot the man in the balls. But the man in the doorway looked at Karen and pointed the pistol at her. The pistol was made out of flesh. It looked like the man in the doorway had a cock growing out of his hand, but it was still a pistol.

"Don't let anyone tell you you can't die in a dream," she told Gavin. "I died."

It was as if Karen were offering an explanation for everything that happened later.

Gavin watches Margaret pay at the counter. All the things he stopped himself from saying are making him anxious, but he is glad he kept his mouth shut. He doesn't trust himself to speak sensibly now. He is too unstable. Sometimes he feels like his strongest emotions have taken on lives of their own and begun battling for control of his life. He sits up straight and rubs the muscles in his lower back, careful not to let his fingers stray too close to the vertebrae. The area above his tailbone is numb again. The sensation produces a hallucination of a negative space opening in his lower back, a zone where the normal laws of physics are reversed, like a black hole in outer space.

Gavin slipped a disc in his lower back four months earlier. *Slipped* is a good word to describe the injury, but it doesn't go far enough. He had been finishing up a renovation job when his lower back started spasming, the muscles slowly gathering into a knotted pinwheel that throbbed at its centre. He should have taken a long break, but he had three guys working for him and would have to hire them for another full day if the job wasn't finished by dinner. If Gavin had been smarter, or if he'd cared less about what his workers thought of him, he would have laid flat on the wooden floor until the spasms stopped. The client wouldn't care. But Gavin didn't want to lie down in front of his crew — they would think he was a flake and use that as an excuse to goof off and stretch the job out another day.

He kept working, promising himself that he would take a week off when this job was over, maybe even take Fiona up to his parents' place for a few days. He bent over to pick up a can of paint and felt a tugging in the back of his legs, then something inside him, what felt like a metal joint connecting his upper and lower body, seemed to slip out of place. His lower body spasmed, then his legs didn't work and he was falling onto the paint cans, only it seemed to take him a long time to fall the three feet to the ground. He felt weightless, disconnected from his body in spite of the pain, or maybe because of it. He fell for a long time.

The doctors kept Gavin on some kind of morphine until the steroids brought the swelling in his back down. He spent most of the next three months in bed, his back at a constant level of pain specially calibrated to trick him into thinking that he might wake up feeling better the next day. Gavin doesn't need to remember the details of that time. He watched a lot of TV. He felt sorry for himself. He worried about Fiona, who had to move in with Margaret and Richard. She had already been spending most of her weekends there since Karen died, so she adjusted. She has gotten used to adjusting. Gavin hasn't. He hated being laid up and didn't try to hide it from anyone but Fiona. At his lowest point he accused Margaret, who brought Fiona to visit every day after work, of slipping antidepressants in with his painkillers and steroids.

What Gavin remembers most about that time is trying to describe, to himself and anyone who came to visit, the exact sensation of the disc slipping out of place. He needed everyone to know not only how much it hurt but how the pain was like nothing he'd ever experienced. A clinical description of the injury didn't explain anything: one of the discs in his lower back had slipped half a centimetre out of place, puncturing the tiny sac of fluid it rested in — breaking a toe on a chair leg sounded more painful. Then Gavin remembered how he felt as if he'd fallen from a great height just after the disc slipped out of place. He began to tell people that it seemed to take at least fifteen seconds for him to hit the ground, as if he'd fallen from a high scaffolding. He kept returning to the image of himself standing on a scaffold two or three stories high. He was on the scaffolding and he took a step back and one of his feet lost its grip and he *slipped*. He tried to regain his balance, but body parts that had been heavy — arms and head and back — were suddenly weightless. His hands leapt for the railings, but he was already falling too fast. The air kept clearing a space for his body, and a long time later he hit the ground. He kept expanding on this analogy until the sensation of falling through a great open space almost replaced the memory of the actual injury.

It bothers him that he spent so much time talking about himself. Worse was that he had dramatized something that had happened to him into a long anecdote in which he played the key role. He had never been the kind of person to tell anecdotes about himself. He has been surrounded by people who tell funny personal stories since he moved to Toronto when he was twenty. His friends have an anecdote for every phase of their life: their first fuck, their first drunk, the day they realized they weren't that young anymore. He enjoys these stories. He's heard them so many times he could tell them himself, but he had prided himself on refusing to learn to speak this specialized language. Now when people ask about the accident he tells them an anecdote. He wonders if this means that he has finally become a Torontonian, but then remembers that most of his friends aren't really from Toronto.

Margaret has already paid for the coffee. Gavin says goodbye to the old Greek man who is watching the CityPulse news channel. Gavin's physiotherapy appointments have been cut to one a week. He still does the exercises, and keeps his apartment clean, and has even started cooking again. There isn't much else to do. There is a permanent scab of scar tissue around the damaged disc; if he tears that the doctors will have to graft a piece of steel between his vertebrae. His insurance will keep him going for another eight months and he has money in the bank, but his contracting business is finished. He has been looking into taking some electrician courses, and in a few weeks he should be able to play the drums again. Gavin knows that he should be worried about the future. He tries to think up financial and personal worst-case scenarios late at night, but his thoughts always grow bored of their mission and evaporate, leaving Gavin on the rim of sleep, remembering how good it felt to fall from a great height.

Gavin is walking down Queen Street. It is one of the first warm days of spring and he can feel the sun softening the expression that has coated his face, like a layer of grease, since the accident. Every morning he sees that same startled scowl in the mirror. The man in the mirror looks as if he has trying to find someone to blame. Every morning Gavin tries to flex his face into a neutral stare or the patient smile of a good retail worker, but it's like trying to will himself to sneeze.

On the street, people linger, feeling the sun, stretching out errands by walking slowly or taking the long route. Gavin looks into the windows of the specialty stores and restaurants and hair salons and feels happy to live in such a busy neighbourhood. He stops in front of the salon where Margaret and Tracy get their hair done and watches a woman with almost silver hair cutting a man's hair. The man in the chair is talking. His eyes are lowered. The man starts to smile, a little embarrassed at what he is admitting, and looks up to catch the hairdresser's reaction in the mirror. The man is probably telling her about a lover he has gotten tired of. The lover wants too much from him. She's always bugging him to stay home at night. If he wanted a wife he would have stayed in his hometown. The hairdresser nods and they meet eyes in the mirror. They might be agreeing on what they don't like in a lover, but they are too coy to reveal what they do like. Maybe they will meet in a bar later and go home together.

Gavin walks away. A woman wearing low-rider jeans and a sweater thinner than most of Gavin's T-shirts passes him on the sidewalk. Gavin watches her tight midriff swelling into the miracle of her hips, and his body seems to rise up and above him like a wave that wants to break on the shores of the woman's back and pull her out to sea. The wave passes over him, leaving Gavin to deal with his restless body, the rows of muscle lying in bulky, ordered folds, desperate for action.

It has already started, the annual sidewalk parade of young women displaying their gym-sculpted bodies in tight but elegant clothes and their freshly scrubbed faces and long straight hair, their good teeth and their bad eyes behind stylishly geeky glasses. The tension gathers in his jaw. His teeth feel alien — wet bones sheathed in soft tissue, weapons lined up in a wet store house. He imagines biting into something firm but yielding and is answered by a phantom pressure in one of his shoulder blades, as if he has just given himself a love bite. For months his body has festered in a swamp of dull aches and shooting pains and bad smells, the swelling in his back a tyrant, his cock a madman locked and raging in a cellar. The sun is out. Everything is waking up. The sharp neutral smell of winter is gone. The dogs on their leashes dangle their tongues.

Gavin walks to the Starbucks next to the yoga studio, though he'd promised himself to stay away. He looks for the girl, knowing that it's still a little early for her to be there. He orders the simplest coffee they have and grabs the sports section from the rack. He reads about the Leafs' chances for the playoffs. The girl — he doesn't know her name — attends a yoga class at eleven on Tuesdays and Thursdays. She comes in after class and orders a tea and reads a Penguin Classic. Last week the book had a piece of ancient pottery on the cover. Gavin can't be more than ten years older — not a huge difference. He's still young enough for more kids.

The girl didn't discourage him the first time she caught him staring. He was only two tables away. She looked back at him and looked down at her book again. She began exaggerating her reactions, rolling her eyes at a boring passage and laughing at another. But because Gavin didn't ask her what she was reading she hasn't encouraged him again. He can still rescue the situation. He only has to pretend to be a little more shy than he really is — Karen used to say that big men can get away with being shy — and start a fumbling conversation that could lead to an invitation to join her at her table.

Gavin doesn't want to speak to her. He wants her so badly that he comes to a public place twice a week to make a fool of himself. But he doesn't want to get to know her. He doesn't want to take her out on dates. He doesn't want to absorb and champion her enthusiasms, or get to know her favourite albums and movies, or meet her friends. He doesn't want to hear her complain about her mother or the guy she works with who keeps hitting on her, and he certainly doesn't want to tell her about his life. He wants to skip straight to her apartment, which he imagines is above a store and is shared with two girlfriends. He wants to fuck her on her lumpy futon while her friends hang out and giggle in the kitchen. And then he wants to watch her sleep.

It's as if Gavin's lust has woken up after a troubled ten-year sleep. He wants the same kind of women he dated before he met Karen: self-absorbed, cocky in public, sentimental in private, newborn downtown girls sprung from small towns or suburbs too narrow to appreciate their quirky beauty. He thought that Karen had cured him of all this, that she had taught him that he could only be happy loving a woman who has outgrown these poses and games. But through some strange loop in time Karen is now the kind of woman that he has been cured of.

Gavin had been determined to make Karen's wake the worst night of his life. Her parents had already paid for a funeral in North York, a location, they said, that would be accessible for the Toronto and out-of-town mourners. The funeral parlour was in an industrial mall near a highway off-ramp. About twenty members of Karen and Gavin's family gathered in a large central room that smelled of roses and something else. There were frosted windows up near the high ceilings, and a lot of armchairs and polished desks and side tables that had never been touched by human hands. Muted ushers materialized from behind strategically positioned palm plants and nodded and gestured the mourners into one of the three chapels. After everyone was seated, a silver-haired man who had never met Karen stood at the lectern and presided over an affirmative, secular ceremony that felt less like a goodbye to a loved one than an initiation into a cult of prolonged numbness. There were things in life we can't understand, he said. Everyone has a different path. Change is the only constant. The man had obviously taken a few courses in public speaking. His synchronized hand gestures carefully unfolded each platitude from its wrapper, displayed it for everyone to see, and then gently placed it back into an invisible box until the next funeral. Fiona did not let go of Gavin's arm during the funeral or the tea and sandwiches that were served in the basement. She looked like a child in the final stages of hypothermia, the last of her body heat making an enraged exit through her unblinking eyes.

The funeral should have been the end of it, but a few days later Margaret told Gavin that "The Community" needed to publicly mourn for Karen, a sentiment that Gavin answered with a long hissing noise.

"That would be the *community* that helped her score the drugs she killed herself with."

"It's not that simple."

"Oh, but it is, it is that simple. And don't forget to invite the *community* that told her to abandon me and Fiona so that she could explore her fucking issues."

"Don't even start on that again, Gavin. You know what she was dealing with."

No, he didn't, or he didn't see how what she was dealing with was any different than what everyone else was dealing with. He was being obtuse. It wasn't that simple. What was simple was that everything had gone wrong. It didn't have to happen this way. Why couldn't someone just say it? He told Margaret to hold the wake if she wanted, but not to expect him to help. He still had to earn a living.

The wake was held in a veteran's hall near Roncesvalles. Gavin and Fiona and his mom arrived at the address, a three-storey grey building that could have been anything — a small warehouse, a biker hangout, or one of those instant Pentecostal churches. The sign on the lawn said "Polish Veterans of the Second World War," though it didn't say which of the two doorways led into the hall. Gavin went around back and found a third door that led into a small bar where about two dozen old men were drinking pitchers of beer and shot glasses of transparent liquor. The woman behind the bar told Gavin that the rental hall was upstairs, but that he had to use the entrance at the front of the building.

He went back to the front lawn. His mom was talking to Fiona and pointing at an old sign painted on the side of a building up the street. The neighbourhood hadn't changed much since the 1960s. Stores were jammed into the bottom floors of houses and the restaurants had plastic plants in the windows. Two streetcar lines converged in a web of cables and rails at an intersection a block away. Everything seemed sealed in an earlier decade by the silver frost and dry cold. Standing there with his mother and daughter, Gavin might have been a man of his father's generation getting ready for a piss-up at the Legion with his buddies. They might have been at a wedding reception for a Polish guy Gavin worked with.

They went through the front door and walked up a

narrow, carpeted staircase. The walls in the stairway were panelled in shiny plywood a little thicker than wallpaper. Someone must have gotten a deal on the stuff. Someone was always getting a deal. For centuries, men had been getting deals on cheap building supplies and pocketing the savings. The pyramids had probably been pannelled in low-grade papyrus that some middleman had gotten at cost from a bankrupt dealer on the Nile. It was a funny thought, but Gavin couldn't laugh with Fiona walking so solemnly beside him in the long, sombre coat Karen had bought for her from a local costume designer. The coat, described by Fiona as "royal blue," was about two sizes too large and had fake fur around the neck and wrists. The sleeves swallowed Fiona's little hands and the contours of her body disappeared under the thick fabric, making her look like an elegant child refugee in an old photo.

Fiona had sworn not to wear the coat until she was "big enough for it," but she'd explained to Gavin earlier that day that the wake would be the only chance for Mommy's spirit to see her with the coat on. A different kind of father would have stroked his daughter's hair and kissed her forehead, uniting father and daughter in a brave front. Instead Gavin knelt down and grabbed Fiona's arm. He was going to shake her and scream that there was no way she was wearing that gaudy coat to the wake. He was going to tear the coat off Fiona and cut it into pieces along with all the self-indulgent, dramatic clothes Karen had bought for her: the little black dresses, the fancy hats, the costume jewellery. Fiona's whole wardrobe had been chosen for a funeral.

Gavin kept squeezing Fiona's arm. He had hardly slept for two weeks. He was starting to see haloes around things. He wasn't always sure if he was speaking out loud or just thinking. For the first time in her life Fiona looked afraid of her father. She tried to back away from him. He couldn't let go, so he pretended that he had almost fallen over and grabbed Fiona's arm for support. To make the story true he forced his hand to slip off her arm and he did actually fall sideways, catching his head on the corner of a chair. It felt like someone had slammed a door shut on his head. It really hurt. He lay on the floor and started to cry. Fiona wasn't afraid anymore. She knelt by her father and said, "Did you hurt yourself, Daddy?" She used a voice normally reserved for frightened stuffed animals.

"Yeah, buddy," he said. "I'm going to have one hell of a lump on my head."

Fiona asked him where and kissed the spot. She seemed to be playing along with his tears, giving him an out, a way of hiding his grief, and for the first time since Karen's death Gavin began to think that he might get through all this.

There were at least a hundred people at the wake. Most of them were social workers and clients from the women's shelter where Karen had worked with Margaret and Tracy. A bunch of the old College Street crowd showed up, many of whom Gavin had lost touch with after Fiona was born. No one from the cheap hotel where Karen spent the last two months of her life seemed to be there. Gavin was disappointed. It would have been fun to throw them down that narrow staircase and count broken bones accumulating like points in a pinball game.

Fiona pulled him toward a table displaying three photo collages of Karen. Gavin tried to blur out his own face when he appeared beside Karen. There was only one picture of Karen and him alone. In the others they were either posing with their friends at a party or a bar or doing something with Fiona — everyone's favourite couple, the quiet guy and the woman everyone was secretly in love with. There were pictures of Karen growing up with Margaret. Even as a child Karen liked stark clothing. Her hair is cut in a severe line across her broad forehead. Suddenly the teenage Karen is dressed all in black, as if there has been a death in the family, and then there are no photos of her until her emergence as the Queen of the College Street scene. Karen is at a bar or a party, the photos too dark or swimming in white light, her friends and lovers trying too hard to match whatever mood has possessed her. They try to be as sexy as Karen, as decadent, as playful, as self-mocking. Her friends and lovers feed on the glamour of her ghostly beauty, her opium-den languor, her recklessness and childish concern for her friends' problems. There are a couple of pictures of Karen at her desk at the shelter, or talking to the women who lived there. He hates the people in the photos. They may not have killed her, but every one of them nudged her closer to death by encouraging her to be a crazy red-haired girl every day of her life.

Eventually Margaret went up on the stage and asked people to say a few words about Karen. One by one, the mourners stood before the microphone. Karen had a "short but vibrant life" that produced "enough memories for three lives." Dozens of endearing anecdotes were told to drive home this point. Everyone put a spin on the last year of Karen's life. They said that she had needed to understand the darkness inside her, inside all of us, making her sound like a cross between a wandering poet and Mother Theresa. A woman Karen had known for about three months, but with whom she had apparently "shared a lifetime," spoke the cliché that Gavin had been dreading all night: "Perhaps now, she has achieved the clarity she could never find in this life." He sat at the head table with Fiona asleep in his lap. He was surprised that Fiona wasn't interested in the eulogies. If he had been in her place he would have lapped up every sentimental pronouncement on his mother's life, but it seemed enough for Fiona to know that all these adults had gathered in one place to say goodbye to her mom.

People say that sitting in Margaret and Richard's kitchen is like being in the country. They call it a "country kitchen," meaning a farmer's kitchen, though most of them have probably never seen the inside of a farm. The original floorboards are intact, and the kitchen sink is deep and lined with pock-marked porcelain that can shatter a plate dropped from two inches. A border of bare wood separates the walls into equal sections, the top decorated with flower-patterned wallpaper, the bottom with white stucco. Margaret and Richard have built matching benches into the corner under the big window and covered the benches with old couch pillows. Fiona loves to sit by the window helping Margaret cut vegetables at the Formica table that Richard found in the garbage and fixed up.

"I could sell that table to a hipster for two hundred dollars," Margaret brags.

Margaret and Tracy do the dishes while Brian wipes off the table and puts the kettle on. Margaret and Tracy are talking about work. Tracy modifies Margaret's accusations about a fellow co-worker without actually disagreeing with her. Richard walks into the kitchen. He is wearing a pair of track pants, a T-shirt, and an old apron with a crest showing a jamboree of cartoon farm animals cavorting under a banner that reads "I Don't Eat My Friends." His hair and beard and apron are coated with tiny spots of paint and dollops of white solvent. For weeks now he has spent his evenings stripping layers of paint from the walls of the small bedroom he is converting into a nursery. Margaret is sure that the bottom layers of paint are lead-based and that the lead, if released into the air, will harm the fetus inside her. "You'd think that we would have learned from the Romans," she says. Richard has to manually strip the paint one layer at a time with an expensive non-toxic, "natural" solvent that Margaret ordered from an on-line store operating out of Vermont. When Richard takes off the apron Margaret spins around as if she has been watching him in a hidden mirror. "Don't take that off in here. The paint gets into everything."

"Yes, mein fuhrer," Richard says. He looks at Gavin, who is lying on the bench resting his back. "My wife, the granola Nazi. Look at me: I inhale all kinds of chemicals at work and I'm fine." He waits a beat to make sure everyone has heard him: "Okay — bad example."

Gavin and Karen used to make jokes about Richard's beard, saying that Margaret forced him to grow it to hide his face from other women. They only joked about the beard when they were alone, Richard's good looks not being on Margaret's list of things that are acceptable to be made fun of. Richard wears unironically clunky glasses and grows his bangs and sideburns long, as if he's trying to draw attention away from his fleshy lips and high cheekbones and slanting green eyes. But Gavin can see the beautiful, alert face behind the vines of hair, watching the world like a half-asleep jungle cat. It's strange that Richard and Karen didn't end up together. They were both so beautiful — looking at each other would have been like seeing their reflections in an enchanted pool. Some law of nature should have asserted itself and forced them to breed more beauty.

Gavin thinks he knows why Richard ended up with Margaret. She weighs him to the earth somehow, demanding that he give her more than what he was born with. The knock on Richard in the old days was that he let women look after him. Margaret is a good-looking woman, though her beauty is too contained, too sober and comforting for Gavin's tastes. The lines of her face are the borderlines and topographical markings on the map of an orderly country estate. Gavin is being cruel, but he can think whatever he wants. He closes his eyes as if to hide what he is about to do. By loosening what feels like the warm handle of a tap in the centre of his chest, Gavin releases a stream of pictures of Karen. If Margaret's face is a map of land brought to order, Karen's was an ancient scroll guiding treasure-crazed captains to their doom, the seas and shorelines of Europe degenerating westward into mermaids and sea-monsters and potato-shaped continents teeming with cannibals and mountains of gold. She had a broad white forehead, and black eyes, and straight red hair.

Gavin once asked Karen what she found attractive about him. She must have been used to men asking her that because she answered with a quick joke: "Besides your nice ass?" She thought about it for a few seconds and then said the first thing that came into her mind: Gavin didn't spend their first date talking about his job or the band he played in. He didn't bombard her with his Very Important Opinions on music or on Quentin Tarantino films. He had asked her about herself, and he listened when she answered. There was more to it than that. Karen loved his body from the start. She always liked big men. Sometimes she would just lie her head on his stomach tracing the muscles in his thighs with her fingertips. She would sigh and say, "Gavin, I *covet* you."

Gavin sits up and opens his eyes. His back is hurting from slouching in the pew at church. The Friday Lenten service usually calms him, but he'd had trouble paying attention. Richard has gone out to the backyard to shake out the apron and take a few tokes. Gavin is glad that Richard makes the effort to keep his habit hidden from Fiona, and that he's cut down to two joints a week since he found out that Margaret was pregnant.

Fiona comes into the kitchen singing to herself. She knows where everything is. She stands on a chair and takes the jar of popcorn kernels from the cupboard and pours the kernels into the hot-air popper. She gets a big plastic bowl to catch the popcorn, and while she waits she makes a kind of waddling motion with her legs and buttocks. She's gotten into the habit of sticking her butt out when she walks, showing off her skinny ass as if it's a Christmas present she just opened. She and her friends take turns doing it and then laugh at each other. They stick out their butts and roll their eyes when boys talk to them and turn everything into a hilarious scandal. Then one of them calls out, "Spy game!" and they run around reminding each other of their secret code names. The next minute one of the girls is shunned for the afternoon and goes home in tears. The girls are trying on the world, wearing its loudest jewellery. Gavin wishes that Fiona's friends weren't so well-adjusted. Their healthy appetites and suspicions, their loyalty and loud displays of emotion seem to turn the natural hierarchy of adult and child upside down — he wants to sit at their feet and learn how to be normal again. But he does everything in his power to nurture Fiona's friendships.

Fiona doesn't acknowledge Gavin. She may not have noticed him sitting on the bench or she may not need to single him out. Fiona's favourite show is on in fifteen min-utes. She won't ask Gavin to watch the show with her. That's Richard's privilege, though Gavin is sure that he would be welcome to join them. He's seen the show. It revolves around a police constabulary in the 1960s and is full of rustic and small-town types with broad Yorkshire accents. Richard comes back into the kitchen and announces in a pan-British accent that he bought a package of shortbread cookies to watch with the show. Fiona takes the package and puts it on a tray with two glasses of milk, then takes a serving dish down from the cupboard. She puts the bowl of popcorn on one of Margaret's breakfast trays and opens the biscuits and arranges them on the serving dish in a swirling pattern. She does all this while mumbling in a singsong voice that is probably her imitation of a servant complaining about the Lady of the Manor.

Since he came off the painkillers a month ago Gavin has been afflicted by sudden attacks of sentimentality. He almost starts to cry when the national anthems are played before the hockey game on TV. The other morning when Fiona was listening to ABBA he got teary thinking about the girl he'd had a crush on in junior high. Watching Fiona's complete surrender to the Friday rituals she loves, he feels his bottom lip start to quiver. He is afraid to exhale too quickly.

When Richard and Fiona are settled in front of the TV, Gavin joins the rest of them at the kitchen table.

"Found this picture," Tracy says.

Brian takes the picture. "Oh, man, look at those mutton chops. Jesus, I look like I just got back from the Boer War."

It is a picture of Brian and Margaret and Tracy at a party. It was taken about 10 years earlier. Brian is wearing a plaid jacket and trucker's cap and sucks in his cheeks and minces his lips. Tracy's hair is dyed almost gold. She is wearing a KISS T-shirt and pumps the air with a beer bottle. Margaret gives the finger in a half-ironic tribute to her former punk-rock self. They were all deep into their irony phase. Everyone Gavin met seemed to play in a band that ended their set with a droll, accelerated cover of a 1970s' hit single. Gavin and Brian's band used to do a medley consisting of an entire side of a K-Tel album called HOT HITS. People went crazy for it.

"Found these, too," Tracy says taking a photo-shop envelope out of her bag. "I've been trying to get rid of stuff before we move next month but I keep finding things that I just can't get rid of." She hands the pictures to Margaret. "But you can keep those."

There are several pictures of Fiona at age four wearing a blue vintage party dress.

"Oh my God, I'd forgotten about these," Margaret says. "Look at her."

The pictures were taken at a house-warming party Brian and Tracy threw when they finally moved in together. Fiona is wowing the party-goers, none of whom had children of their own, with her precocious observations and sassy comments. She organized a game of hide-and-seek that the adults took far too seriously. There is a picture of Fiona exhausted in Karen's arms. Karen has cut her hair down to half an inch.

Gavin had forgotten about the haircut. Fiona freaked when she saw Karen without her long straight hair. She said that Karen wasn't her real mom. She said to Karen: "You're not fooling me." Even after Fiona accepted that this nearly bald woman was really her mother she kept on at Karen to grow the hair back. Karen assured Fiona that her hair would grow back, but she would not be consoled: Fiona wanted her mom's *real* hair back, the hair she had cut off. Fiona offered to build a time machine — she'd seen how to do it in a movie, you just had to build a car that could go backwards fast enough. Karen cried when she heard that.

When Gavin saw Karen for the first time with short hair he thought that she'd been arrested, thrown in the psych ward, had her head sheared, and been let out on a day pass. He'd been expecting her to do something crazy. She had been making cryptic comments about "feeling trapped" and telling Gavin that she wasn't good enough for Fiona and him. She said it all had to do with the things she was remembering about her childhood. He asked if that was why she cut her hair and she said that there was no reason, she'd just gotten sick of looking at the big auburn "dog ears" that hung down on either side of her face.

Gavin wanted to tell her that he didn't know if he could love her without her hair. Her eyes, formerly the natural centre of her face, holding her oversized mouth and tiny nose in proportion, now dominated and amplified her expressions, as if every smile or pout were the beginning of a revelation. Looking at her face laid bare he asked himself for the thousandth time how such a beautiful woman could love a man as ordinary as him. With her hair cut, Karen looked even more like a faerie, a creature no mortal man could hope to love.

"Don't you like it?" she asked.

He told her that it made her head look big.

"My head?" she said. She was always telling him what a big head she had.

"I liked your hair."

"So did I. That's why I cut it."

"That's so fucking retarded."

They both started laughing. That was the last time one of their arguments ended with laughter and sex.

Gavin must be holding the photo for too long because the kitchen has gotten very quiet. Tracy and Margaret and Brian have all found neutral surfaces to stare at.

"I can't believe she cut her hair," Gavin says.

He expects more tense silence, but Tracy surprises him. "She was always mixing things up," she says. "Now, what you've all been waiting for." Tracy shows them the yearbook she has brought home from Wilson. "Do you want to see me in Grade 8?" She opens to a page near the end of the book.

"You would have been cute if it weren't for the glasses," Brian says.

"Aren't they great? But don't forget about the hair. I look like a boy."

Gavin easily finds Tracy in the rows of stamp-sized photos. She does look like a boy — an earnest builder of model ships, a devourer of science fiction novels. He wonders if Fiona will go through an awkward phase when she hits puberty. She won't. She is too confident, too good-looking. She has noticed that boys her own age are starting to show off and compete for her attention. Their behaviour irritates her, but she is beginning to accept it as part of the natural order. In a couple of years she will notice the power her body has over her male teachers and the men who leer at her on the streets and subways.

"How come all the boys look like they've just gotten away with a crime?" Margaret asks, looking down the rows of photos.

"Because they probably have."

Gavin imagines a line of cars following Fiona as she walks home from school, the drivers leaning out of the windows to check out her ass and tits.

Tracy angles the book so that they can all see the pictures. "Look, there's Wanda. It was about this time that she stopped believing that she was a horse. And Dan, the toughest kid in the school, used to cry every time he got a spelling test back. He used to get like two out of twenty-five, but he could drive a transport truck by Grade 9."

"My God," Margaret says. "That was the age of velour and corduroy. With velour you could always tell who owned a pet because they came to school covered in fur."

Tracy turns the page. "Cindy Thomas: rudest girl in the school. I hope she's in jail but I think she's teaching children. That's Robert LePage. After burning down his parent's house he lost his licence for DWI. Cindy Moriarity: got pregnant, works in the box factory now." There is no maliciousness in Tracy's voice as she reads off her former schoolmate's life sentences. She sounds like a judge who wishes the sentences she is handing down could be more lenient. "God, poor Wanda — I believe she works with flowers now. Sheila: she was the first girl to get breasts."

"Edie Palmucci, Grade 6," Brian says.

"Terry Mackenzie, Miss Beaton's homeroom class," Gavin says. The names come to the two men instantly, though they haven't given the girls a thought in twenty years. The crushing mystery of an annoying tomboy sprouting breasts over the summer. Gavin remembers Terry Mackenzie trying to fold her breasts back into her body as she walked the gauntlet of the boys' desperate, assessing stares. What will he say to Fiona when she comes home crying, telling him that the boys won't stop watching her? What will he say to her when she says that all boys are pigs? He will agree with her and tell her to avoid them. He will rage against the boys who are forcing Fiona to be ashamed of her body, but knowing Fiona, she will ask him if he used to stare at girls' breasts at school. He knows what he'll say, that his parents taught him to respect women. He might have wanted to stare, but he knew better. He'll tell her the same sort of lie when she asks him about drugs and drinking, creating an image of himself as an ideal teenager in the hopes that she will seek out such a boy to love.

Tracy points to another Cindy, condemned to night shifts at the box factory, a doll fetish, and an apartment above her parents' store. Cindy Number Three: "Pregnant, dropped out of school. There's Tracy Neville again. She looks like a boy here, but now she's living in Toronto on the hippest stretch of College Street."

"And has a boyfriend who plays in a band," Brian says.

"I heard that she's become an evil feminist," Margaret says.

"Who wears trousers on Sunday!"

"Michelle Tanner: once the queen of the playground,

caught doing cocaine at her first wedding. She drives a truck now and is living in Manitoba with a boyfriend she shares with her mother. Joey Anderson: owns a restaurant. Bobby Harris: don't know what's happened to him since he got caught masturbating at work."

"No!"

"Oh yeah, he just whipped it out at his desk and started spanking away. He had a desk job," Tracy says, as if this is the story's most surprising detail.

"Good for him!" Brian says.

"Obviously no one taught him about work site decorum," Margaret says. It's hard to tell when Margaret's joking, which makes her rare bursts of humour even funnier.

Brian does a dead-on Northern Ontario accent: "Jeez, eh, no one fucking told me I couldn't pull out on the job. I was on my fucking break!"

Gavin is laughing so hard that he has to hold onto his lower back with one hand. "How come I don't know all this stuff about the good citizens of Parry Sound?"

"Because your mom isn't the town gossip." Tracy has turned to the teachers' page. "Mr. Kendall: ate garlic to take the smell of booze off his breath. That's Mr. Tucker, gym teacher and coach of the girl's soccer team. Also known as Ron Tucker, Athlete Fucker."

Margaret laughs so suddenly that she has to spit some of her tea back into the cup.

"It's true," Tracy says. "He liked to leave the first three buttons of his shirt undone and invite some of the stars of the girls' sports teams for a ride in his sports car."

Gavin will be keeping an eye on Fiona's male teachers. He straightens his back. In a few months he might be able to start working out. The doctor said he can start doing some laps in the pool next week.

"Miss King: kept kleenex in her bra. Never could figure

out why — she had big hooters. Mr. Gilmour: had a nervous breakdown in class on the first day of school in my final year. Mr. Scott: married one of his students." She turns the page and runs her finger slowly over the last two rows of teachers. "Drunk. Closet gay. Wrote romances under a pseudonym. Communist. Lesbian."

"Ah, she must have been the gym teacher," Brian says.

"Actually, she taught English. Ms. Ferguson. She's probably the only reason I made it out of Wilson. She told me that I was too good for Wilson."

"I had a teacher who said I was too good for Mississauga. Name was Coach *Don* Tucker, Boy-Athlete Fucker," Gavin says. "Said with my lips I could be pulling in two grand on a Friday night in Toronto."

"Have you seen Ms. Ferguson since?" Margaret asks.

"Once. We went out for a drink one summer when I was visiting my parents. I think I was in university. Evening didn't go well. She thought I'd gotten too big for my britches."

Gavin is in the kitchen waiting for Fiona to brush her teeth and get into her nightie. She used to insist that Gavin get ready for bed at the same time as her, but now she does it alone. She told Gavin that she was "almost going through puberty" and had to learn to do things in private. Remembering this, Gavin sees the same image of a teenage Fiona walking home from school, only now he is the man stalking her in a car, cradling a crowbar in his right hand, watching for men in the alleys and doorways and other cars.

Richard is cleaning up in the kitchen while Margaret and Tracy and Brian have a smoke in the backyard. "You can crash here if you want," he says.

"Well, if I fall asleep I won't bother getting up."

"Sounds like a plan."

Fiona comes into the kitchen in her housecoat and gives Richard a long hug good night. As always, Richard is surprised by the depth of Fiona's feelings. He rests his hands on her shoulders and makes an in-joke with her in a bad Yorkshire accent. He will make a good father.

"Where's Auntie Maggie?" Fiona asks.

"Smoke."

"Cancer!"

"I'm trying to get her to quit," Richard says.

Gavin walks upstairs with her. When they get in her room she starts to play a game, jumping from one pile of clothing to the next. "My feet are tied together and I'm only allowed to step on the clothes," she says. "The rest is lava. I have three life points. If I step on the lava I lose half a life point. Do you want to play? It's a fair game."

"Back's kind of sore." That's his answer to everything these days. "Come on buddy, you're supposed to be winding down. How are you ever going to get to sleep?"

She looks at him and rolls her eyes, but as soon as she is under the blankets she seems to lose about four years. She says that she needs him to lie down with her until she falls asleep. Last year Gavin asked Margaret if Fiona needed someone to lie down with her when he wasn't there. He wasn't surprised that the answer was no. It's as if Fiona only remembers that she's afraid of the dark when her father is around. Maybe this is what Karen meant when she said that Fiona would be better off without her.

Gavin turns off the overhead light and switches on the little lighthouse night light beside the door. Fiona occasionally walks in her sleep, a habit that Gavin dates back to Karen walking out on them. When Margaret asked about it, he said that Fiona had always been a sleepwalker. He doesn't want anyone making the connection.

He lies down on the bed and Fiona lays an arm across his chest.

"Daddy, you won't ever leave me, will you?"

"Buddy, where did that come from?" He tries to sound casual, mildly concerned, but this is the question he has never wanted her to ask.

"I want you to move with me when I live in Alexandria."

"Jeez, what will I do there?"

"You can help me dig for Cleopatra's palace. We'll live there and have a summer home in the tropicals of Africa."

"I guess," he says. "It sounds like a good plan. But you have to get your degree first."

"Daddy, I know that. That's why you're putting money in my school fund."

"Yes," he says. "That's right."